Grimmtastic Girls

Snow White Lucks Out

Grimmtastic Girls

Grimmtastic Girls

Snow White Lucks Out

Joan Holub & Suzanne Williams

Scholastic Inc.

No part of this publication may be reproduced, stored in a retrieval system, or transmitted in any form or by any means, electronic, mechanical, photocopying, recording, or otherwise, without written permission of the publisher. For information regarding permission, write to Scholastic Inc., Attention: Permissions Department, 557 Broadway, New York, NY 10012.

ISBN 978-0-545-51985-4

12 11 10 9 8 7 6 5 4 3   14 15 16 17 18 19/0

Printed in the U.S.A.   40
First printing, July 2014

For our grimmazing readers:

Sofia G., Kaitlyn H., Isabella F., Izabel K.,
Prisca M., Megan D., Micaila S., Lily-Ann S.,
The Andrade Family & Alba C.,
Khanya S., Christine D-H., Mona P.,
Lorelai M., Abby G., Jasmine R.,
Caitlin R., Erica H-F., and you!

~ Joan and Suzanne

Contents

It is written upon the wall of the Grimmstone Library:

Something E.V.I.L. this way comes.
To protect all that is born of fairy tale, folk tale, and nursery
rhyme magic, we have created the realm of Grimmlandia. In
the center of this realm, we have built two castles on opposite
ends of a Great Hall, which straddles the Once Upon River. And
this haven shall be forever known as Grimm Academy.

~ The brothers Grimm

1

Fake

Snow White's Grimm Academy handbook slipped from her fingers and hit the hallway floor with a smack. "Oh, hobwoggle!" she exclaimed as she bent to pick it up. Stuffing the handbook into the sparkly blue school bag that hung over her shoulder, Snow shut the lid-door of her trunker — a fancy leather trunk that stood tallwise on its end and opened like a locker.

The trunker key that hung from Snow's silver necklace clinked against a round crystal amulet as she pulled up on the chain that held them both. There was a four-leaf clover inside the amulet. Although it was the luckiest among her collection of good luck charms, its luck wasn't working for her today. She had accidentally missed her first class!

And now Snow was running late for second period. All because she'd spent *hours* lying awake last night and worrying that *some* people were suspicious of her loyalty to the Academy. A little spear of hurt stabbed her as she glanced over at the trunker two down from hers. There was a small heart-shaped picture on it of a girl with red-streaked, curly black hair, wearing a hooded red cape. Her so-called BFF, Red Riding Hood. It was all *her* fault Snow had overslept today. Ever since Red had started hanging out with a boy named Wolfgang, she'd started acting funny around Snow, like Snow couldn't be trusted. It was so not fair — especially since, in Snow's opinion, Wolfgang didn't seem very trustworthy himself!

Quickly, Snow poked her key into the trunker's lock and chanted the locking part of her combination. "Nine, ten, a-big-fat-hen!"

Snick! As the lock snapped into place, an image of Snow's face magically painted itself in the small heart-shaped inset on the trunk, right above the lock. Short, neat, ebony hair. Pale skin with rosy cheeks, and green eyes.

She slipped her key back out of the lock and dashed down the first floor hall of Pink Castle, where the girls of Grimm Academy lived and had most of their classes. There were hardly any students around the halls as Snow raced toward the grand staircase to get to Threads class. Most everyone else was already *in* class.

A mere dozen feet from the stairs she heard a familiar sound. *Click. Click. Click.* It was the sound of high heels on the marble steps.

"Oh, no!" she muttered, screeching to a dead stop. Snow's stepmom, Ms. Wicked, was coming down the stairs. Her favorite handbag hung over her arm and she held a rolled up piece of vellum paper in her hand. She was probably heading for her classroom on the first floor, where she taught Scrying — the art of using crystal balls and other reflective surfaces to predict the future.

Hoping her stepmom wouldn't look up and see her, Snow leaped to hide behind a tall stone column. Unfortunately, she tripped over one of her shoelaces mid-leap. Standing with her back against the column, she looked down to see that her lace had broken. Had her stepmom seen her stumble? Snow held her breath, staring at the lush scene of feasts and pageantry woven into the tapestry on the hall wall across the way. If only she could wish herself inside of it so she could *really* hide. But they wouldn't learn how to do that kind of magic in Threads class till next year.

Click. Click. Click. The footsteps came closer. "Snow! Come here!"

Talk about unlucky! Her stepmom had spotted her after all. High overhead, carved gargoyles grinned down at Snow from the top of a column farther down by the trunkers. Although she would rather have faced a real, live gargoyle, Snow obediently stepped out from behind the column.

"Hi," she said, giving her stepmom a weak grin.

Ms. Wicked frowned with disapproval. Typical. It was the expression she almost always wore whenever she looked at Snow. "I just spoke with Ms. Queenharts," Ms. Wicked snapped in an accusing tone. "She told me you were absent from Comportment class this morning."

Snow gulped. "Oh, yeah. I overslept," she explained. Honestly, she hadn't minded missing Comportment. Ms. Queenharts was terrible at teaching manners!

Her stepmom's dark eyes narrowed. "If you're trying to get more beauty sleep, it's not working, sweetie." She looked Snow up and down and pointed the end of the vellum roll she held toward Snow's ankles. "Also, the hem on that gown is way too short. Your ankles are showing and they aren't exactly your best feature."

Just then, Prince Hunter and Prince Awesome walked by on their way to class. Had they heard her stepmom's criticisms? How grimmbarrassing! Snow felt a rosy flush creep up from her neck and spread over her entire face.

But Ms. Wicked sent the passing students a beautifully sweet smile. *Why is she nice to everyone but me?* Snow wondered. It made her feel so . . . inadequate. She could never figure out which part of Ms. Wicked's personality was the real one. The smiling, beautiful one? Or the mean, critical one?

Bong. Bong. Bong. The Hickory Dickory Dock clock over in the Great Hall echoed throughout the school, signaling the hour and the start of second period as well.

Snow started sidling toward the grand staircase. "I . . . um . . . I guess I'd better head off, then." She reached with one hand to tug at the hem of her gown, though it wasn't all *that* short. In fact, if it were any longer she'd be tripping over it. Speaking of tripping, she did just that — again. Drat that broken shoelace!

"Oh, dear. You're a mess this morning, aren't you?" Her stepmom gave Snow another of her patented disapproving looks. Then, she tucked the roll of vellum under one arm and reached into her stylish handbag.

After rummaging around in it for a few seconds, Ms. Wicked pulled out a brand-new pair of shoelaces. Pretty blue ones that matched Snow's dress, no less. It was amazing what she could conjure from that bag! Although it was a normal-size bag, she was always pulling out just the thing you needed from it. Even things that were way too big to fit inside.

Ms. Wicked sent Snow a dazzling smile as she handed her the laces. "Here. Use these. They'll work like magic."

"Thanks," said Snow. Instances of kindness like this had always made it impossible for her to truly dislike her stepmother. Still, she felt a bit wary as she accepted the shoelaces. Her stepmom's gifts didn't always work out. Like the earrings she'd given Snow on her tenth birthday. They'd made Snow's ears grow twice as big as normal when she wore them. And then there was the time her stepmom had given her a music box that had made Snow dance for hours, until Red had happened to come along and rescue her by shutting it.

As Ms. Wicked closed her handbag, the vellum roll she'd been holding fell to the floor and unrolled. Snow knelt and picked it up, her gaze taking in the drawing of the crystal ball on it and some of the words written below:

> *The Crystal Maptracker is capable of locating secret treasure maps . . .*

Snow rose slowly, a feeling of dread creeping over her as she realized what she held. It was an order form. For a map-finding crystal ball. There was only one secret treasure map Snow had ever seen personally. It was a mapestry, a magical map in the form of a stitched tapestry that showed all of Grimmlandia, including the Academy. And Snow and her friends, Red, Cinderella, and Rapunzel, had it!

They'd secretly discovered it at Prince Awesome's ball a few weeks ago. They hoped it would lead to a legendary treasure so enormously rich that it might save the school from a terrible, secret society called E.V.I.L. — as in Exceptional Villains In Literature. It was a society her stepmom belonged to. And it looked like she must be trying to find the treasure, too!

"I'll take that," Ms. Wicked informed Snow, snatching the vellum sheet and tucking it under her arm once more. Then she stepped aside and flicked her red-polished fingertips toward the stairs. "Run along now, sweetie. Wouldn't want you to get detention for missing your first class *and* being tardy to your second." Heels clicking, she swept down the hallway.

Yikes! I'm going to be really late now! Snow realized. Which was partly her stepmom's fault. Putting the order form out of her mind, Snow stuffed the new laces into her schoolbag and raced up the stairs. As she pushed through the door to the second floor hallway, she tried to shake off the familiar feelings of uncertainty and embarrassment that settled over her after every such encounter with her stepmom.

Those feelings had colored her entire childhood. No matter how small the offense, her stepmom still had the power to make Snow feel like a misbehaving three year old. *But, hello?* She was twelve now. She shouldn't let her stepmom's put-downs get to her. Yet she did.

Snow slid through the classroom door as the last *bong* of the school clock died away. She hardly noticed when her fingers rose to clasp her lucky amulet. It was something she automatically did when she felt the need for a little extra luck.

"Sorry I'm late," she murmured to her Threads teachers, Ms. Muffet and Ms. Spider. She started toward her seat.

Ms. Muffet's knitting needles kept on clacking as she smiled at Snow from the yellow satin-covered tuffet she was sitting on at the front of the room. "Don't worry. You're fine," she said.

"Phew! Close call," Snow muttered under her breath. Her fingers slid from the amulet. If only her stepmom were as easygoing as Ms. Muffet!

Spotting one of her BFFs, Rapunzel, at the back of the room, Snow skirted a loom where a girl named Goldilocks sat sorting through a basket of yarn for a difficult project she was weaving. "This thread is too thin, but this other one is too thick," Goldilocks said in a frustrated tone. "And this is too blue, and that's too purple. None of it is quite right."

But then along came Ms. Spider, who sat down beside her to help. The teacher quickly sorted through the basket, selecting some cobwebby threads. As Goldilocks watched, Ms. Spider began to weave them over and under the warp so deftly that it would seem to anyone as if she must have at least eight hands rather than the usual two.

Rapunzel, a goth-looking girl with dark brown eyes and long, glossy, blue-streaked black hair, smiled at Snow as she sat down next to her. Her hair was woven in loose, thick braids that almost touched the floor.

"Didn't see you at breakfast," Rapunzel said. "What hap —"

"Overslept," Snow explained before Rapunzel could finish asking.

Rapunzel simply nodded, not making it into a big deal. Then her dark-red-glossed lips curved up on one side and she looked at Snow uncertainly. "So what do you think?" she asked, holding up the black stocking she was knitting.

"Nice," said Snow, studying it as she pulled her sampler out of her school bag. It was on the tip of her tongue to suggest that Rapunzel add some color to the stocking, like a zig-zag row of pink or some sparkly silver, for example. But she didn't. Rapunzel liked black, and that was fine for simple stockings. No way did Snow want to be critical like her stepmom.

Rapunzel paused her knitting needles and peered at Snow's sampler in surprise. It featured cross-stitched alphabet letters bordered by red and pink hearts and roses. "You finished your project already? You're so fast."

Snow shrugged. "Thanks." She'd finished it last night while worrying over possible reasons for Red's recent unfriendliness. It was on the tip of her tongue to ask Rapunzel if she knew why Red had been acting suspicious and standoffish. But maybe she'd only make things worse by asking. Or Rapunzel might just say she was imagining it. Even worse, Rapunzel might *agree* that Red didn't like her anymore!

Should she at least tell her about the map-finding crystal ball her stepmom was ordering? It was something all of

Snow's BFFs would want to know about. They'd be as worried as she was that Ms. Wicked might use it to get their mapestry, which she'd then use to try to locate the treasure. But what if telling her friends about the order form made them wonder if Snow had let something slip that had given her stepmom the idea of finding the treasure to begin with? She didn't want to make Red even *more* suspicious of her ability to keep mum. Maybe she would wait a bit. In the meantime, she'd try to find a way to stop her stepmom's plans by herself.

"How do you make your stitches so even?" Rapunzel asked, giving Snow's sampler an admiring glance. "It can't just be because you've taken Threads every year since first grade. Because I have, too, and I still stink at it."

Snow grinned. "I inherited my talent from my mom. She was good at embroidery, too. Just before I was born she told my dad she hoped they'd have a daughter with skin as white as snow, lips as red as blood, and hair as black as her ebony sewing frame."

"Her wish came true," said Rapunzel, sending Snow a fond smile.

Snow nodded as she rose and went to turn in her completed sampler to Ms. Spider for grading. Next, she stopped by the supply closet and cut a square piece from the long roll of open mesh canvas. She also grabbed a box of assorted needlepoint twist thread at random. She wished her mom had been around when she was growing up to teach her sewing. And other stuff.

Instead her mom had died when Snow was less than a year old, and that's when her dad had married Ms. Wicked. Then, when Snow was only six, her dad had died, too. Afterward she and Ms. Wicked had been booted out of the castle by a distant male heir. Her stepmom had had to take a job teaching at the Academy to get by. Thing was, she *could* have put Snow in an orphanage. But to her credit she didn't. Was it a (mostly hidden) streak of kindness that had made her keep Snow with her? Or did Ms. Wicked just like having her around to criticize? Snow had never really figured it out.

Snow took her seat again and glanced over at Ms. Muffet, who was patiently helping a girl named Polly unsnarl a huge pile of red yarn. "Sometimes I wonder what it would be like if one of the other teachers at the Academy were my stepmom," she confessed to Rapunzel.

"Yeah, like Ms. Muffet or Ms. Spider," agreed Rapunzel. "Think of all the great clothes they'd sew for you!"

Snow's emerald-green eyes sparkled as she threaded her blunt needle with blue twist. "Or how about Ms. Goose? She's so much fun and knows the most awesome stories. And she can make up rhymes about anything in half a second." Ms. Goose was the school librarian, and she also composed most of the locking code rhymes for the trunkers.

"Hey, and maybe she'd teach you to fly around the library on her goose," said Rapunzel.

Snow grinned and began pulling her blue-threaded needle through the mesh cloth from back to front. She didn't really have a design planned out, but she often worked by instinct. Once a design began to form, she would simply go with it.

"Of course, my stepmom's not so bad," she added after a minute, feeling a little guilty. "I mean, she can be kind of critical, but that's only because she wants what's best for me."

Rapunzel's eyebrows rose, but she said nothing. *Clack, clack* went her needles. As the stocking she was knitting grew, so did her hair. The tips of her braids were touching the floor now, Snow noticed. Rapunzel had to cut her fast-growing hair almost every day.

Snow's blunt silver needle flashed in and out of the cloth. The area of blue stitches grew wider on her needle-point design.

"How come you decided to use invisible thread?" asked Rapunzel after some time had passed.

"Huh?" Snow looked down at her needlepoint. She'd already sewn a big blue patch. Couldn't Rapunzel see it? Then she noticed something intriguing. Her fingers had sewn the blue in the winding shape of the Once Upon River, which the Academy building straddled. Without thinking about it, she had begun to sew a map. But not just any map. Unconsciously, she'd started to copy the magical treasure mapestry they'd found!

Hmm. What if she could make it convincing enough to fool even her stepmom into believing it was the *real* mapestry? She smiled inwardly. It was a brilliant idea. One that might just save the whole school!

2

Prince Prince

Snow glanced down at the box of needlepoint twist she'd gotten from the supply cupboard. Its label read:

> *Invisible Twill Thread. Making a gift to surprise a friend? Only the one who uses these spools (or magical helpers in his or her employ) may see what the final project will be . . . until the last stitch is sewn.*

"I picked up a case of invisible thread by accident!" Snow told Rapunzel. Only now she was glad she had. Because no one but her would know what she was making until it was finished.

Luckily, the clock began to bong, distracting Rapunzel from the needlepoint. Good thing, since Snow wasn't quite ready to reveal her plan for it. She stuffed it into her bag as the girls said farewell, and headed off in different directions to third-period class.

Snow pulled up on the silver chain around her neck as

she started down the steps to the first floor again. At the bottom, she paused behind an enormous column and waited until the final warning bongs were about to sound. Then she gave her clover amulet a kiss for extra good luck, and sprinted down the hall. Up ahead, she saw Red's friend Wolfgang dart out of her History class and into her stepmom's classroom next door. She was pretty sure he had Drama this period with Red up on the third floor. So what was he doing down here going into Scrying? Acting suspicious, that's what! Why would he be visiting Ms. Wicked?

Snow's amulet came through for her, and she made it to her Grimm History of Barbarians and Dastardlies class without her stepmom coming into the hall. *Hooray!*

Oops! Her luck quickly ran out. Just as she went into the classroom, Snow tripped and stumbled forward over the threshold. She plowed right into Mr. Hump-Dumpty!

Thwump! They both went tumbling to the floor. The oval-shaped egg-teacher dropped the snazzy walking stick he always carried. And something else, too. She only caught a glimpse of it as it went skittering across the room, but it had looked kind of like a wooden ruler — about a foot long and straight.

"Oh, dear, what a scramble!" wailed the teacher, who was rolling around on his back. His legs, which ended in long, pointy shoes, kicked in the air as he tried to regain his balance.

Unhurt, Snow leaped up and grabbed hold of one of the teacher's arms to try to pull him up. However, he was so roundish and heavy that she couldn't quite get him onto his feet. "I'm so sorry! I forgot that one of my shoelaces is broken," she explained in a rush. "That's why I . . ."

Before anyone else in the class could come to their aid, a boy she'd never seen before appeared beside her. A very *cute* boy. He wore a crown, which meant he must be a prince.

"Got it," he told her and took hold of Mr. Hump-Dumpty's other arm. Between the two of them and some other students who gathered around, they finally managed to stand the teacher upright. Then the prince retrieved the teacher's walking stick and held it out to him.

"Thanks for the *eggs*tra help, Prince," Mr. Hump-Dumpty said to the boy.

"No problem," said the prince. His blue eyes flashed in Snow's direction for a second, and then he went to take a seat.

There were lots of princes and princesses at the Academy. Snow herself was a princess since her dad had been a king, her mom a queen. Royalty didn't impress her. But this boy's kindness and his cuteness kind of did!

She looked around for the wooden ruler thing she'd seen go flying and finally found it under Mr. Hump-Dumpty's desk. Now she saw that it wasn't a ruler after all. Though long and straight, it was also round. And it had holes along its length. Once she fished it out and handed it to him, she realized that the holes were *finger* holes. It was some kind of wooden flute.

"Where did this come from?" he asked, eyeing it curiously as he took it.

"Um. Your jacket?" she replied, pointing. Duh, didn't he recognize his own stuff? "I'm really sorry I tripped you, Mr. Hump-Dumpty. It's just that I broke one of my shoelaces, as I was saying. I've got replacement laces, though. So I'll switch out the old ones right away."

"*Eggs*ellent. *Eggs*actly the kind of safety-preparedness I would *eggs*pect from you, Snow," he said. Absentmindedly, he tossed the flute onto his desk.

Despite his easy acceptance of her apology, the incident must have rattled him. For as Snow went to sit down at a double desk in the middle of the classroom, he launched into a lecture full of warnings about accidents waiting to happen and precautions one should take to avoid them. Snow sat down and pulled out the blue shoelaces her step-mom had given her just that morning.

"Is he always such a worrywart?" asked the boy who'd helped her stand the egg-teacher back on his feet. The other side of her double desk had been empty since the new school year had started, but as luck would have it, the new prince had taken it!

Snow nodded, setting the laces on top of her desk for now. "Yeah. He's more chicken than egg sometimes." The

17

prince grinned at that, and she went on, pleased he'd gotten her little joke. "So you must be n —" Before she could voice her question, her roommate, Jill, whose twin brother Jack also attended the Academy, caught her eye from one row over. Jill pointed at the prince and wiggled her eyebrows, giving her a thumbs-up.

Snow blushed. She obviously hadn't been the only one to notice how cute this new boy was. Golden hair. Sparkly blue eyes. Straight nose. And dimples, too, she noted when he smiled at her. "You must be new, right?" she asked him in a low voice so Mr. Hump-Dumpty wouldn't notice them talking.

"Yeah. Name's Prince," the boy said, keeping his voice low, too. "Principal R introduced me to everyone in the Great Hall this morning, didn't you hear?"

"Oh, sorry, I missed breakfast." She idly wound a shoelace around one finger, then looked at him again. "You know, we've got a lot of princes at the Academy, so most just go by their last names."

The boy grinned. "Okay. Then you can call me Prince."

She cocked her head, more than a little confused. At the front of the room, Mr. Hump-Dumpty's dire warnings and suggestions for how to avoid fearsome things like paper cuts, stubbed toes, and skinned knees petered out. He turned toward the whiteboard at the front of the room and began to write a reading assignment.

"Prince *is* my last name," the boy explained quickly. "It's my first, too. A little weird, I know."

"So your name's Prince Prince?"

When he nodded, she said, "I'm Snow."

"Yeah, I know," he told her. When her brows went up in question, he nodded toward Prince Foulsmell, who also had History this period. "I asked Foulsmell who you were when you came into class," he informed her.

Huh? Why would he do that? she wondered.

By now, Mr. Hump-Dumpty had stopped writing. Turning toward the class again, he tapped the tip of his walking stick on the board, where he had written in big block letters:

BEWARE OF TRICKSTER FAIRIES

"Please open your handbooks to chapter four," he said crisply.

Prince leafed through the blank vellum pages of his book. "Um," he said to Snow. "Speaking of trickster fairies, I think one of them must have got hold of my book and erased all the words inside it."

Snow shook her head. He must not have needed his handbook during his earlier classes, or he would have learned how it worked already. "Your book's contents change depending on the class. Here, watch me," she whispered.

She pressed a finger to the oval in the very center of her handbook's cover where the scrolly, entwined *GA* — for Grimm Academy — was printed. At the same time, she said, "Grimm History of Barbarians and Dastardlies."

Prince copied her. "So *that's* how it works," he exclaimed when he opened his book and saw that it was now filled with words.

Both of them quickly found the beginning of the fourth chapter, which was titled, "A Brief Guide to Grimmlandia Fairies." What followed were descriptions of various fairies such as pixies, dwarves, flower fairies, elves, and other wee folk.

Some types were categorized as *helpful*, like the hardworking dwarves who were talented at metal-working, mining, and crafts. Others were classified as *harmful*, like tricky leprechauns, who often pretended to lead people to treasure while instead getting them lost. Helpful, harmful, villainous, or heroic — all fairy folk and characters from fairy tales and nursery rhymes had been given a home here within the walls of Grimmlandia. The two Grimm brothers, Jacob and Wilhelm, who'd actually written many of the tales, had seen to that.

As everyone read the chapter silently, they touched various words in their handbooks. With the press of a finger, bubbles rose with animated figures or information inside them. Snow pressed on an illustration of a cute cottage, causing a group of seven dwarves, each about five inches tall, to pop up in a bubble. Seven was her lucky number!

Quickly, the bubble burst and the dwarves became three-dimensional. Hopping out of her handbook, they began scurrying around in different directions and tidying up her desk. When they finished that task, she meant to press on the cottage illustration again to put them back inside their bubble. But before she could do it, four of them grabbed the new blue shoelaces she'd set on her desk. After jumping to the floor, they began swapping out her old laces for the new ones.

"Thanks," she told them, having momentarily forgotten about doing the task herself.

As the dwarves worked on her laces, Mr. Hump-Dumpty started a discussion, asking students to argue for or against the helpful or harmful labels. Snow's hand shot up. In her opinion, these dwarves were certainly helpful! Class flew by after that. Suddenly, the Hickory Dickory Dock clock was *bong*ing the half hour to end third period, its deep voice emerging from a grate high on the wall at the front of the room.

"Class dismissed!" Mr. Hump-Dumpty called out.

Snow looked down to see her shoes neatly laced and the dwarves gone. She hadn't even gotten a chance to thank them. She quickly stashed her handbook in her sparkly blue school bag and went to the door. There, she poked her head out into the hall and checked both ways. No sign of her stepmom. She stepped one newly laced, blue-slippered foot out into the hall, hoping to escape while the coast was clear. She didn't need any more critiques of her clothing today, thank you very much.

As it turned out, she wound up walking right beside Prince on the way toward the Great Hall. "Are you walking me to lunch?" he asked her curiously, after they'd gone a half dozen steps.

"Nuh-uh," she said truthfully. Because they weren't exactly *together* or anything. Just accidentally walking side by side. But then it occurred to Snow that if he was with her and they happened to run into her stepmom, her stepmom would act nicer than if Snow were alone. At least a little bit nicer. So she stuck by his side. It was kind of awkward actually, because neither of them said anything for the whole length of the hall. Luckily, they reached the stairs without running into Ms. Wicked.

Feeling a bit embarrassed by now, Snow dropped back as they took the stairs. However, Prince waited for her at the bottom. Soon they were side by side again, heading for the Great Hall.

"Are *you* walking *me* to lunch now?" she quipped with a grin.

He flashed her a grin in return. "Maybe." Then he drew a silver coin from his pocket and began flipping it in the air and catching it as they walked. "I wanted to ask you some-thing. Um, where's Battle Science class?"

"Over in Gray Castle somewhere." Why was he asking her? she wondered. Mostly boys took that class, so it was located in Gray Castle, where the boys' dorms were. "You should ask Prince Awesome or Prince Foulsmell exactly where. They both have it, I think."

"Oh, yeah, good idea," Prince said. But for some reason, he made no move to catch up with those two boys, who were up ahead. Did that mean he really wanted to walk with her? On purpose? He flipped his coin high, and then caught it neatly as it fell. "Compared to Foulsmell, Prince isn't such a bad last name, huh?" This time he caught his coin behind his back after he tossed it up. "Because you have to admit Foulsmell is a little . . ."

"Foul-smelling?" Snow supplied. "Just his last name, though. Not him," she added, in case Prince thought she was saying that Foulsmell himself was stinky.

"Right. He's cool. Awesome is, too. They're both in my Sieges, Catapults, and Jousts class second period." Prince tossed his coin in the air again. But this time it got away from him. After clanging against the stone column they were passing by, it went skittering down the hall back the way they'd come. Snow scooched up against the column to get out of the way of other students while Prince ran after it.

"Coin! Come!" he called to it. Immediately, it circled

around and rolled back to him. He scooped it up in his palm and jogged back to her. "Phew," he said, looking a little embarrassed as he pocketed the coin. "Sorry to be so dramatic, it's just that this coin is sort of, well . . . *lucky*."

Snow smiled, thinking it must be magical, too, since it had come when called. She lifted up her silver chain to show him her amulet. "I have a whole collection of good luck charms," she confided as they continued walking. "But this is my luckiest. The four-leaf clover inside belonged to my mom."

According to a story Snow's dad had once told her, her mom had been convinced that the clover had brought her good luck. Because shortly after she'd found it she had discovered she was going to have a baby. And that baby had been Snow!

"What else is in your collection?" Prince asked, appearing genuinely intrigued.

She named a few things, like her dad's brass button and her lucky mustard seed. "Last year in Threads, I even embroidered a sign that says: *Luck Comes to Those Who Are Prepared.* It's hanging on my armoire," she told him.

"Hey! My dad says that all the time," the prince said in surprise.

"Really?" asked Snow, pleased. The motto was one she lived by, *preparing* herself with as many good luck protections and rituals as she possibly could. She loved that her mom had believed in luck, too. But at times she wondered about the nature of luck, considering that her mom had *died* soon after Snow was born. So many bad things had happened in her family that in her lowest moments, she sometimes wondered if she herself might be an *unlucky* charm. Still, just as her mom had, she truly believed that good luck charms could ward off bad luck.

After a minute, things got quiet and Snow realized they'd stopped in the hall and were now just gazing at each other. She started walking again, and the prince did, too.

"What's your lucky number? Mine's two," said Prince, as they entered the Great Hall. It was enormous and beautiful, with a balcony at either end, rows of windows with diamond-shaped glass panes, and colorful banners lining the walls.

"Seven," Snow told him happily. Not even her three BFFs had ever asked her that question. Finally, here was someone who shared her enthusiasm for all things lucky!

Speaking of BFFs, she looked around and waved to Rapunzel, Cinda, and Red. They were already seated at their usual place at one of the two long tables that stretched down either side of the Hall. And they'd saved her a spot.

Up ahead, someone waved to the prince from the lunch line, shouting, "Prince! Over here! I saved you a place in line since it's your first day and all!" It was Foulsmell.

"See you later," Prince said to Snow. "If I'm *lucky*!" With a laugh, he went to join Foulsmell and some of the other boys farther up the line.

Mistress Hagscorch looked extra grumpy today as she served up portions of her divine nine-day-old pease porridge pot pie and her pigweed salad.

Snow hadn't had much for breakfast, just a couple of oatmeal cookies from the cookie jar in her dorm's common area, so she was super hungry. She stared at the delicious food and tried not to drool.

"Hold up your tray, I haven't got all day!" the crabby cook barked at her.

Snow gave a little jump. She had been so intent on the food that she hadn't realized she was next in line. She stared into Hagscorch's scary eyes, which were as yellow as a cat's, and said, "The pot pie looks *sooo* grimmazing today. Could I please have two servings?" Normally, she wouldn't have dared ask. Almost everyone was at least a bit afraid of Hagscorch, including her.

But to Snow's surprise, a huge smile broke out on the cook's craggy face. "That's what I like," she cackled. "A girl with a good appetite. Keep eating like this, and I'll fatten you up in no time!" A wrinkled old hand shot out and pinched her cheek. Then Hagscorch plopped a plate with a double-serving of pot pie and a huge mound of pigweed salad onto Snow's silver tray.

Woo-hoo! It was her lucky day, or lucky lunch, anyway!

3

The Pipe Swipe

Carrying her heavy tray with its overloaded plate, Snow went to sit with her three BFFs. Now that she studied all the food she had, though, she wondered if her eyes had been bigger than her stomach would turn out to be.

"Was that the new prince you came in with?" Red Riding Hood asked before Snow could even sit down. As usual, Red was wearing her hooded red cape over a tunic and skirt. The hood was pushed back, revealing her dark curls with glittery red streaks running through them. Beside her on the bench sat a cute nut-brown wicker picnic basket with swirly designs on both ends, double handles, and a hinged lid. Red seldom went anywhere without it.

Snow nodded. "He was in my History class last period." As she set her tray on the table, Red quickly scooted over to make room for her on the bench. Her basket scooted over, too, and snuggled up to Red's side. It was her *magical* charm — which was not at all the same thing as a lucky

27

charm — and could fetch things if asked in just the right manner. However, it would only obey Red.

Cinda had a magical charm, too — a pair of glass slippers — but Snow and Rapunzel had yet to receive their charms. Most students went to the Academy for months or years before their special charms appeared.

Snow was relieved that Red was not looking at her with eyes full of suspicion, as had happened so often lately. Instead, all three of Snow's friends were staring in amazement at her heaped plate.

Rapunzel sent her a teasing smile. "Hungry much?" she joked, making Snow giggle.

Red spread her arms wide, and gestured toward Snow's tray. "Behold this magnificent feast!" she exclaimed in a dramatic voice. "Did I not say the king would provide for you? Through my efforts his bounty shall be shared with all, though he does not like it. Yet try as he might he cannot stop me from my *thievery* of his goods." As she spoke the word "thievery," Red snitched a forkful of pigweed from Snow's plate, and wolfed it down. Then she half-stood and gave her three BFFs a mock bow, grinning at her own silliness, before sitting once again.

Snow smiled as she dug into the delicious pot pie. Ever since Red had gotten the lead role of Red Robin Hood in the school play a few days ago, she'd begun to spout lines from it whenever the fancy struck her.

"Bravo," said Cinda, clapping. Snow, Red, and Cinda all roomed in the same dorm — Pearl Tower. It was one of the three turrets at the top of Pink Castle. Rapunzel, however, roomed in the dungeon. By herself. By choice. She was afraid of heights and rarely climbed to the dorms. Snow could've chosen to live with her stepmom in the teachers' quarters. *But, uh, no thanks!* It was way more fun rooming with the other girls.

"So how are your practices with Wolfgang going?" Cinda asked Red.

Red blushed, smiling slightly. "He's been giving me lots of good pointers. And I've given him some." Wolfgang was the male lead in *Red Robin Hood* and the star of last year's school play. Snow strongly suspected that he and Red were crushing on each other. Even if they didn't know it yet!

"Rapunzel said you overslept this morning," Cinda said, switching her attention to Snow. "Second time this week. What's up?"

"Nothing," Snow said, after swallowing another bite of the pot pie.

Red's eyes sharpened on her with suspicion. *Oh, no, here we go again*, thought Snow. So she'd been late to class. Big deal. What did Red think Snow had been up to — doing evil deeds for her stepmom instead of going to class? As if!

Not seeming to notice the tension between them, Cinda smoothed back her candle-flame yellow hair. "So I guess you heard there'll be a ball this coming Saturday," she said to Snow. "In honor of the new prince, Prince Prince. Which means . . ."

"New ball gowns!" all four girls chorused together.

"Prince Prince," Rapunzel mused, her lips curving upward. "Kind of a confusing name."

"Maybe he needs a nickname," Cinda said thoughtfully.

Snow paused with a forkful of crunchy pigweed salad halfway to her mouth. "Like Principal R?" GA students had tons of nicknames for Principal Rumpelstiltskin, though they never said them to his face. Names such as Stiltsky, the Rumpster, and Grumpystiltskin. It was against rule 37 in the school handbook to say his real name. Besides, saying it would make him throw a terrific tantrum, though nobody knew why. *He* couldn't even say his own name without sparking a fit.

Feeling a slight tickle on her ear, Snow reached up to scratch it. But the scratching didn't ease the itch. Was she having an allergic reaction? She examined her pigweed salad more closely. It had a faint, lemony taste. There wasn't any real lemon in it, she hoped. She never ate lemons. Because she was very allergic to fruit.

According to superstition, which Snow put much store in, an itchy ear meant that someone was talking about her. She'd certainly prefer that to an allergic reaction! She looked around, and her eyes fell on Prince Prince at the far end of her table. He was talking to Prince Awesome. About her? No, that was dumb. Why would they talk about her?

When both boys happened to glance her way at the same time, Snow quickly pretended to be studying a group of four bluebirds that was swooping overhead in the Hall. The birds must've thought her gaze meant she was trying to signal them that she had finished her lunch. Instantly, they zoomed down and each took a corner of her tray in their beaks. They lifted it away before she could stop them!

But maybe that was a good thing, in case there really had been lemon in the salad. Since even thinking about fruit could bring on an attack of hiccups or worse, she focused on what her friends were saying instead of what she'd eaten. They'd begun to discuss their plans for a festival to earn money for the school, and Snow joined in the conversation. "We're so lucky Principal R actually approved our idea," she said.

"Luck, schmuck," Rapunzel said, speaking her mind. "He's desperate for funds to keep the Academy going. Has been ever since Peter Peter Pumpkineater's pumpkin was stolen from the library."

"True," said Snow. The pumpkin contained the Seeds of Prosperity, which meant that the school would fail to prosper unless it was found and returned.

"That pumpkin's probably gone forever," said Red. "Off to the land of beasts and dastardlies."

Snow nodded. The girls had helplessly watched the pumpkin change into a stagecoach, roll off into Neverwood Forest, and eventually go over the wall that surrounded Grimmlandia. Beyond that wall was the Dark Nothingterror. It was a place no one had ever visited and lived to tell about it, according to Mr. Hump-Dumpty. Though now that Snow thought about it, how could anyone really *know* what happened to visitors that went there, if they never came back to tell?

It was also said that terrible beasts and dastardlies roamed the Dark Nothingterror. But even after years of History class, Snow wasn't sure what a *dastardly* was exactly. Still, she knew she didn't ever want to meet one!

Cinda took a long sip of her patty-cake shake. The yummy sweet and syrupy drink was one of Ms. Hagscorch's special concoctions. Snow eyed it hungrily, wishing she'd gotten to eat more of her lunch after all.

"Too bad Grumpystiltskin can't just sell off a few of the school's tapestries or statues to solve our money problems," Cinda went on. It was something they'd all bemoaned before. But Rule 8 in the Grimm Academy Handbook stated that the sale of school property was forbidden.

"Yeah, and too bad Jack and Jill's magic fire pail went missing, so he can't continue with his alchemy experiments for fear of burning down the school," said Rapunzel. "Not that there was any *real* chance he'd succeed in turning anything to gold," she added.

"This is Grimmlandia," Snow protested. "Magic *does* happen."

Rapunzel looked skeptical. "But all Principal R's and Ms. Jabberwocky's alchemy *magic* has produced is burned-up, sizzling, useless bits." Ms. Jabberwocky, the principal's fire-breathing dragon lady assistant often helped out with his experiments. Or at least she used to.

Cinda leaned across the table to speak in a quiet voice. "I heard that the school's finances are in such bad shape that it might have to close at the end of the year."

Snow felt herself turn even paler than usual. Where would she go if the Academy closed? To live someplace else with her stepmom probably. No more living in the dorm with her friends. Her heart thumped with panic. "If only we could find the treasure, and —"

"Shh," warned Red. "We can't let *Them* find out about the *You Know What*."

"Oops. Sorry," said Snow, clamming up. *Them* was the four Grimm girls' code-speak for the E.V.I.L. Society, and *You Know What* was code for the magical mapestry. The mysterious and villainous Society had existed around the time the Grimm brothers founded Grimmlandia, but it had later died out. For some reason, it had recently begun to operate again. And now it seemed bent on weakening the magical wall around Grimmlandia that had kept all the fairy folk and fairy-tale and nursery-rhyme characters within its borders safe for more than a century!

"Speaking of which, who has the *You Know What*?" Rapunzel whispered, her eyes scanning the other three.

"Me," said Red. She patted her basket's lid, which was firmly closed. The girls all took turns guarding the mapestry. At the first ball of the school year, Cinda's glass slippers had danced her over to the spot where it had been hidden under a loose tile right here in the Great Hall.

"So any new clues to report? Golden blobs? Moving stitches?" Cinda asked Red.

The mapestry could unexpectedly change itself at times, with new stitches appearing and disappearing. They hoped it would eventually lead them to the legendary treasure long rumored to be hidden somewhere inside the walls of Grimmlandia. No one knew what the treasure was, but Snow was sure it must be gold and jewels. Finding it would solve the school's money problems. *As long as my stepmom and the Society don't find the treasure first*, she thought with a shudder, remembering the order form she'd seen.

When Red shook her head, Cinda drained the last of her patty-cake shake. "So where should we meet after school? Upstairs in the dorm?"

Out of the corner of her eye, Snow saw Rapunzel cringe. Snow gestured toward the windows and blue skies beyond. "It's a beautiful day," she said quickly. "Why don't we meet by the swan boats and paddle out to Maze Island instead? It's more private than the dorm." Maze Island was in the middle of the Once Upon River. If they met there, Rapunzel wouldn't have to climb up to Pearl Tower, and they wouldn't have to worry about anyone overhearing their treasure-hunting plans.

For a second, Red's brow furrowed at the suggestion, like she was suspicious about why Snow had suggested they meet at the island instead of in the dorm. *Honestly!* Snow was becoming more and more certain that Red didn't trust her at all. Maybe Red didn't even *like* her. It was confusing. And besides that, it *hurt.*

But then Red's brow smoothed. "Okay," she said slowly.

"Yeah," said Cinda. "Good idea. We can check out the repairs since the big alchemy accident."

"Perfect," Rapunzel said, sounding relieved.

As the girls finished their lunches, Snow kept sneaking peeks at Red when her attention was elsewhere. The girls all knew that Snow's stepmom was connected to E.V.I.L. Was it really possible that Red doubted Snow's loyalty because of that?

It wasn't fair! Cinda's stepsisters, Malorette and Odette, were part of E.V.I.L., too — they'd even been the ones responsible for stealing Peter Peter Pumpkineater's pumpkin. And how about that suspicious-acting Wolfgang? Was there any real proof that he wasn't part of E.V.I.L.? Yet Red still trusted both him and Cinda.

Impulsively, Snow touched Red on the arm. "You don't think I —"

Just then trumpets blared. *Ta*-ta-ta-*ta*-ta-ta-*tum*! Everyone in the Hall jumped in surprise at the sound. Snow glanced up at the two musicians who had appeared in the west balcony.

"Attention, scholars," chorused five shiny iron helmets behind them. They sat upon a wide, carved wooden shelf high on the stone wall at the back of the balcony. "The great and goodly principal of Grimm Academy wishes to address you!" The helmet-heads, each topped by a different-colored feather, comprised the GA school board.

All the students rose and turned toward the balcony. "I wonder what this is all about?" Snow overheard Red's roommate, Gretel, say from somewhere behind her. Snow was wondering the same thing. Principal R always made announcements in the morning, hardly ever at lunch.

Stomp! Stomp! The principal began to climb a stepladder that was situated behind the railing of the balcony. First his tall hat appeared, then his long nose and long-chinned face, and finally the rest of him. He was a gnome. Three feet tall at most.

Though he was scowling, Snow couldn't really tell if he was unhappy. He pretty much always looked a bit, well, grim.

Wasting no time, he got right to the point. "Students of Grimm Academy! This morning during first period another valuable artifact was stolen from the Grimmstone Library!" he announced. Like all gnomes, he had a surprisingly loud and commanding voice that practically forced you to perk up and listen.

Red held up three fingers and silently mouthed to her friends, *That makes* three.

Snow nodded. Peter Peter's pumpkin had been the first artifact to go missing. Jack and Jill's pail, the second. What was missing now?

"It was a pipe," the principal announced flatly.

He must be really *upset,* thought Snow. Because usually he'd ask students to *guess* what the item was instead of telling them outright. She pictured a piece of metal plumbing and tried in vain to figure out what story or nursery rhyme it was connected to. *Pumpkin. Pail. Pipe,* she mused.

And all three are Ps, she mouthed at her friends. Was that a coincidence? Or —

"You mean like a drain pipe?" a student dared to ask.

"No!" blasted the principal.

"The kind of pipe you smoke?" another student asked. Snow looked over to see that it was Prince Prince.

37

"No! A musical pipe," Principal R explained testily as if that should have been obvious.

Oh! thought Snow. That *kind of pipe!*

"The Pied Piper of Hamelin's musical pipe to be exact. It's made of pearwood, and it's about this long." Principal R held his hands about twelve inches apart to show them the pipe's length.

Snow gasped. *Huh?* It had suddenly dawned on her that Principal R had just described the flute that had flown out of Mr. Hump-Dumpty's pocket when she'd plowed into him in History class. *Flute. Pipe.* Two names for the same thing!

"It must be found!" The principal leaned forward. "Can you guess why?"

Students threw out random guesses, knowing he'd expect them to. "Because it plays a song you want to hear?" "Because it'll steal all the music in Grimmlandia?" "Because you're starting a band and need a flute?"

"No. No. And absolutely not!" the principal replied, dancing around with glee. He loved it when no one could guess the answer to his questions. Then he stopped and leaned so far forward that he was in danger of falling out of the balcony. And he told them the answer.

"Because it's capable of luring other magical objects out from under our very noses!"

4

Good Egg, Rotten Egg

*E*veryone in the Hall gasped at Principal R's revelation.

Since the E.V.I.L. Society members are the ones doing all the artifact stealing, does that mean Mr. Hump-Dumpty is a part of E.V.I.L.? worried Snow. He'd certainly *looked* startled when she'd handed the flute . . . er . . . *pipe* back to him. Was that because he'd felt guilty for taking it?

"If it escapes, the wall around Grimmlandia will be dangerously weakened," the principal was saying. "I must warn you all again to be on the lookout for suspicious activity. And if you know anything at all about this most recent theft, I expect you to report to me at once!" He doffed his hat. "Good day, scholars!" With that, he stomped back down the steps.

Ta-ta-ta-*ta*-ta-ta-*tum*! Brightly colored flags with the GA symbol on them unrolled from the trumpets' long, slender stems.

As the musicians finished and the students sat down, the Hickory Dickory Dock clock over in the east balcony at the Pink Castle end of the Hall spoke up:

39

"Hickory Dickory Dock,
The mouse ran up the clock.
The clock strikes noon.
Fourth period starts soon.
Hickory Dickory Dock."

When the rhyme ended, a mechanical mouse popped out of a little door above the clock's face, which had eyes, a nose, and a mouth. The mouse squeaked cutely twelve times to signal noon. Its squeaks were followed by twelve low-toned bongs that echoed throughout the Academy.

As bluebirds flew down to pick up her friends' silver trays, Snow finally got a chance to speak up. "I know something," she began.

"I hope so," Rapunzel teased. "Otherwise all those classes you've been taking for years would be a waste of time."

"Ha!" Snow made a goofy face at her. "I meant that I know something about the pipe. I think." Quickly, she explained what had happened in History class.

"But Mr. Hump-Dumpty is a *good* egg," Cinda protested. "Isn't he?" She dipped her fingers into a little silver bowl of water that a bluebird had returned to set before her, then wiped her hands on a clean white linen napkin.

"Yeah," Red agreed. She held out a handful of table crumbs for the bluebirds that were servicing their table. "It's hard to believe he might actually be *rotten* enough to steal an artifact. Maybe the pipe you saw was his, not the stolen one."

"Only, I don't think he's musical. Have you ever heard him try to hum a tune? He's really off key," Rapunzel commented as she, too, fed the birds. "Besides, he's so quick to see danger everywhere and to warn us about hazards to our lives and health. Doesn't seem likely he'd dare put his lips on a pipe belonging to someone else for fear of getting germs."

"I hate the idea of ratting him out. But . . . what do you think I should do?" Snow asked anxiously as the girls rose from their table and headed to their fourth-period classes.

As she slung her blue bag over her shoulder, it seemed to wiggle a little. *Huh?* She quickly dismissed her curiosity over this, however. The things inside — her handbook, the fake mapestry she'd just begun to sew, pens and paper, lip gloss, and spools of thread — must have shifted. That was all.

Cinda sighed. "We never told Principal R about my two stepsisters stealing Peter Peter's pumpkin. But maybe we should try trusting him with a little information, and see what happens."

"Not a bad idea," said Red. "Snow could tell him she saw something that looked like the missing flute in Mr. Hump-Dumpty's room and then let Principal R decide what it means. And when we see what he does, it'll help us know if he could be part of E.V.I.L., too."

"Good plan," said Rapunzel. She glanced at Red and Cinda. "Let's go to his office now. If we wait, we might get too freaked out to do it later."

"You'll go with me?" Snow's spirits lifted. Rapunzel must have realized just how much she dreaded facing the principal alone with her news.

"Of course," said Cinda. "One for all and all for one, right?"

"If we stay long enough, I might even be late for fifth-period Calligraphy. Yes!" Red pumped a fist at the thought of missing part of her least favorite class, and the others laughed. Snow was in that class, too, but she liked it!

"Thanks," said Snow. "You guys are the best." She hoped that Red felt the same way Cinda did about their friendship.

They headed toward Pink Castle and took the stairs to the fourth floor, where the the principal's office was located.

When they climbed up beyond the third floor, Rapunzel grasped the railing tightly, hyperventilating a little. Snow gave her arm an encouraging squeeze and stayed beside her as they went up that last flight to the fourth floor. Given Rapunzel's fear of heights, it had been especially brave of her to volunteer to come along.

Ms. Jabberwocky stood up from her desk, which was covered with paperwork, when the girls entered the office.

"Callooh! Callay! It's the Grimmble girls!" She smiled at them, showing her enormous, sharp dragon teeth. Although she meant to be friendly, her smile was actually rather scary. All four girls took a small, nervous step backward.

"I hope she's already had lunch," Snow heard Rapunzel murmur under her breath.

"What can I do for you brillig girls today?" asked the dragon lady.

Cinda cocked her head, looking a little confused since she'd only come to the Academy recently. However, Snow and the others were used to Ms. Jabberwocky's odd way of speaking. Her occasional nonsensical words came from an ancient language once spoken by dragons.

"We're here to see Principal R," Snow announced.

Ms. Jabberwocky's scaly face twisted into a concerned expression. "Does he know you're coming? He's in an uffish bad mood. All these frumious thefts, I suppose. Plus, he misses his frabjous alchemy experiments." She glanced wistfully at a half-eaten jar of jalapeño peppers sitting on a corner of her desk.

She must miss doing alchemy, too, thought Snow. Ms. Jabberwocky had always provided the fiery heat for the principal's experiments with her jalapeño pepper and hot sauce–fueled breath. Until the recent ban on unnecessary fires after Jack and Jill's pail went missing from the library, that is.

"We've come about the stolen pipe," Red announced. She elbowed Snow.

"Yeah, I saw something," Snow blurted.

Suddenly, the door beyond Ms. Jabberwocky's desk — a door marked PRINCIPAL R'S OFFICE — burst open and the principal himself appeared. "I heard that!"

Has he been listening at his office door? Snow wondered. Eavesdropping because he didn't have enough to do now that his alchemy experiments had been halted? If so, perhaps he needed a new hobby!

The principal dashed toward the three girls, and leaped onto Ms. Jabberwocky's desk to stare down at them. "Well? Speak up! Tell me what you know!" he boomed at Snow.

Quickly, she explained about the pipe, saying she'd seen it on Mr. Hump-Dumpty's desk. She told how it matched the description Principal R had given everyone at lunch, leaving out the fact that it had originally fallen out of Mr. Hump-Dumpty's pocket. As she spoke, Principal R's arms twitched, his eyebrows rammed together, and his nostrils flared. She hoped he wasn't working himself into another of his famous tantrums.

He stayed relatively calm until the end of her story. But then he exploded. "Dagnabbit!" he roared. Purple-faced, he whirled around like a small tornado, making a stack of papers atop Ms. Jabberwocky's desk go flying. As she zoomed around trying to catch them all, he came to a sudden halt. Tapping an index finger against his long chin, he looked thoughtful. "If staff members are involved in the recent thefts around here, things are really getting bad," he mused to himself, seeming to forget the girls for the moment.

If staff members are involved? Snow traded surprised looks with her three BFFs. *Was it possible he knew less about E.V.I.L. than they did?* Because they already knew for a fact that at least one teacher — Ms. Wicked — was involved with the Society.

"There's no proof that Mr. Hump-Dumpty really stole the pipe, though," Snow told him anxiously. The girls all liked the egg-teacher. That's partly why coming here to talk to the principal about this was so hard.

Principal R frowned. "His guilt or innocence isn't something you need to worry about. But tell no one else what you've told me. Just rest assured that I *will* get to the bottom of this, or my name's not Ruh — Rum —" The principal thrust his fists under his arms and began taking deep breaths, in and out and in and out, as if trying to bring himself back under control. As his eyes bulged and his face began to turn purple again, Ms. Jabberwocky took charge.

"Visit's over, Grimmble girls," she sang out, setting the stack of pages she'd rescued back on her desk. She handed them late slips so they could get into their fourth-period classes. As usual, the passes were a little burnt around the edges. Without further ado, she whisked them out into the hall with a cheery, "Better make like mome raths and gyre on back to class!"

She slammed her office door shut and then reopened it saying, "Oh, and have a *happy ever afternoon*!"

Wham! The door shut again.

"Phew," said Cinda as the girls headed downstairs. "Grumpystiltskin can be really *intense*."

"No kidding," said Red.

"Ms. Jabberwocky's not exactly relaxing to be around, either," added Rapunzel.

"Yeah, especially if you're a can of hot sauce or a jalapeño pepper. Gulp!" said Snow and they all giggled. A warm feeling filled her, almost as if she actually had gulped hot sauce herself. Because for this one moment she was able to shove aside her troubles and just let the familiar good feelings she used to feel between her and her friends flood through her. No suspicion. Just shared laughter.

As the girls moved down the hall, Snow thought about the mapestry. So far, they'd kept it secret from Principal R. For one thing, they suspected he'd take it away from them if he knew they had it. It was so awful not knowing if they could trust him entirely. They didn't *think* he had anything to do with E.V.I.L., but time would tell.

At least they could trust each other — except for Red not altogether trusting Snow! A little dart of sadness pierced her at the thought. Maybe once she finished the fake mapestry and gave it to her stepmom to keep her from searching for the real one, Red would truly believe Snow hadn't spilled any secrets or gone over to the E.V.I.L. side!

When the girls reached the first floor, they pushed through the stairwell door and started down the circular hall toward the classrooms. Cinda and Rapunzel had History together now, and Red was right next door in Ms. Wicked's Scrying class.

"See you," Snow told the others as they peeled off for their classrooms. Then she continued along to Balls class in the Great Hall, which would already be half-over. She hoped she and her friends had done the right thing in talking to the Stiltsky. He could get so angry! Would he fire Mr. Hump-Dumpty without a fair investigation of the matter and kick him out of the Academy? Or even worse, fry Mr. Hump-Dumpty in one of his *fiery* alchemy experiments in spite of the fire ban? If anything like that happened, she'd feel terrible!

Automatically, Snow's hand went to her lucky clover amulet, and she made a wish. "If Mr. Hump-Dumpty is innocent, please protect him." Then she added, "Even if he's not, please don't let him get fried."

5

Kicking It

Music greeted Snow's ears as she pushed through the ornate wooden doors to the Great Hall. These doors were kept open during mealtimes, but were closed during dance classes so as not to disturb other classes in session. Up in one of the end balconies, a small group of musicians with wooden recorders of various sizes were playing a lively tune for a dance called the galliard. The dance involved a lot of hops, leaps, and kicks, which made it great fun, in Snow's opinion.

The two long dining tables had been shoved against the walls to create floor space in the middle of the Hall for dancing. Snow watched for a few minutes as several boy-girl student pairs hopped and kicked their way forward together while holding hands, then dropped hands to circle each other.

Ms. Eight, one of the twelve Dancing Princesses who took turns teaching Balls class, clapped out the five-step rhythm of the dance as the students practiced. Today, she wore eight wildly patterned scarves, had four earrings in each ear, and her bangs were plastered flat around her forehead and temples in exactly eight stiff curls. The rest of her long reddish-brown hair was wound into a tidy bun at the back of her head that had eight decorative hairpins stuck in it.

"Right. Left. Right. Left. Cadence," she called out repeatedly as she clapped along to the music. "*Won*-derful! *Love*-ah-ly!" She and the other Dancing Princesses were famous. They gave performances all over Grimmlandia in addition to teaching at the Academy.

Once the song ended, the dancers went to sit on the floor, and another group took their place. Snow's interest perked up when she saw that Prince Prince was among them. So they had two classes in a row together. Grimmtastic!

Before the music and dancing could start again, Snow sidled up to Ms. Eight and handed her the pass Ms. Jabberwocky had given her. "Sorry I'm late," she said.

Ms. Eight tossed the slip of paper onto the nearest table with a graceful fling of her arm. "No worries, *dah*ling. It's spec-*tah*-cular to have you here at *lahst*." She nodded toward the five students who had moved onto the floor. "We've been one girl short. Now you can *pahrt*ner with the new student, *dah*ling. How *faaa*bulous!" She gestured at Prince Prince.

"Okay," said Snow. But as she moved toward Prince she suddenly felt a little shy. Sitting beside a boy or walking down a hall next to him was one thing. Dancing with him was another.

For some reason Prince looked a little stressed out, too, as she approached him. "Boy, am I glad to see you," he said. "I hope you know how to galliard."

"I do," she assured him. She gazed around at the other pairs of students. "Who were you dancing with before I got here?"

"The teacher." He rolled his eyes as if that had been the worst thing imaginable. Lowering his voice, he went on. "Everyone else knew each other and paired up right away. And nothing against Ms. Eight, but she likes to lead. So I had to dance the *girl's* part." He grinned.

Despite the grin, he seemed really relieved to have a new *pahrt*ner, um, partner, Snow thought. Until that moment, she'd never considered how hard it must be to start at a new school where you knew no one and no one knew you. Students usually gravitated to their friends whenever they had to pick partners, so Prince had to be feeling kind of left out. Cinda was new to the Academy, too, but at least she'd started on the first day of the new school year. And she *did* have stepsisters here, despite their awfulness. Snow had never gone to school anywhere but the

Academy, and, of course, her stepmom was with her when she started. Determination filled her to help make this new prince feel welcome.

The musicians began to play, and Snow offered Prince her hand. "I'll lead you to the dance floor, but I promise not to lead you after that, *dah*ling." Her cheeks flushed when she realized what she'd just said, that she'd called him darling. She'd only meant it as a joke because Ms. Eight called everyone that. But had he understood? She hoped he didn't think she'd actually meant the endearment seriously. *Argh! How grimmbarrassing!*

Fortunately, Prince didn't seem to notice anything amiss. He simply took her hand in his. As Ms. Eight clapped to the rhythm and called out the steps, the group began to hop and kick their feet in time to the music. Almost immediately, Snow tripped.

"Gotcha!" said Prince, hardly missing a beat as he swung her around.

"Thanks for the rescue!" she told him. If not for him, she might've done a face plant! Prince nodded and dropped her hand to circle behind her. She stayed in place, kicking and hopping while also concentrating hard on staying upright. But then, as they executed the next move, she tripped again! What was up? "Sorry, I really do know this dance, and I'm not usually so clum*seee*!" There she went again — falling.

"Maybe try focusing on something other than your feet," suggested Prince. "Like, um, talking. Tell me why you were late to class."

Snow hopped around to the beat, not knowing what to say. She and her friends had agreed not to talk about E.V.I.L., and she could hardly explain about the pipe and the girls' visit to Principal R without bringing up the Society. Or poor Mr. Hump-Dumpty. "I . . . uh . . . had to run an errand for my stepmom," she lied as she executed a kick. "Ms. Wicked, that is."

Prince's blue eyes widened. "Ms. Wicked is your mom?"

"My *step*mom," Snow corrected him just before he started to circle her again. Though she did feel some family loyalty toward Ms. Wicked, she thought it important for Prince to know that the two of them weren't really related, in case he took a dislike to her stepmom. On the other hand, Ms. Wicked oozed charm to everyone except Snow, so he'd probably like her just fine.

"I have her for first-period Scrying," he said once he'd circled her and they'd joined hands again. "Must be nice having family right here at school. I'm going to miss not seeing my parents and sister every day."

What could she say? That if she and Ms. Wicked weren't here at the Academy together she wouldn't miss her step-mom one bit? He might think that was weird. And maybe even mean of her. So she kept mum.

"Right. Left. Right. Left. Cadence," Ms. Eight chanted.

On her next kick, Snow suddenly lost her balance. "Whoa!" she cried. As she fell backward to the floor, she pulled Prince down, too. They just sat there for a minute, staring at each other in surprise. After checking to see that they were all right, Ms. Eight went to speak to the musicians.

As soon as she left, Prince jumped to his feet, then pulled Snow up after him. "Are you really okay?" he asked her.

"I'm fine," Snow told him, blushing. "I'm so sorry. Guess I'm just having a clumsy day today. Starting with History class. At least I didn't knock over the teacher this time."

"No, just a poor lowly prince." He executed a bow. "But feel free to knock me over anytime."

Snow laughed again. She wasn't exactly sure, but it seemed like Prince was *flirting* with her. If so, she kind of liked it.

Suddenly, she noticed something fly in through one of the Hall's enormous windows. As it sailed overhead a high trilling sound came from it. "What's that?" she asked.

Prince looked up, too. "A bird?"

Snow shook her head. "No, it's too long and thin."

"A flying ink pen?" he joked.

"It's playing music." She gasped, realizing what it must be. "The Pied Piper's pipe!" she shouted, pointing up at it. All dancing stopped as everyone stared upward. The musicians in the balcony ceased playing to stare up at the pipe, too.

"There's something following along behind it," said Prince as another small object flew in the window.

"A chess piece — the queen I think," said Snow. And then came a ruby ring. The two objects were trailing the pipe.

"It's like they're playing follow the leader," someone noted.

But where was the pipe leading them?

Bam! Just then, the double doors to the Great Hall burst open. Principal R and Mr. Hump-Dumpty came running in. A group of students including Cinda and Red, as well as Ms. Wicked and several other first-floor teachers, also followed.

"There it is! Get back down here, you pesky pipe!" shouted the principal, shaking his fist at it.

The pipe ignored the principal's summons. When it did several twirls and loop the loops near the ceiling, the ring and chess piece copied it. The pipe was playing such a lively and merry tune that Snow halfway wanted to fly up there and follow it, too!

As the objects zoomed by overhead, a silver spoon appeared from the kitchen, hovering in mid-air. It did a little spin and then floated up to join the end of the line following the pipe. Then a silver dish came along and did the same. Almost as if this is what the pipe had been waiting for, it abruptly zoomed out a window on the opposite side of the Hall. The line of four objects followed it out of view.

Ms. Hagscorch ran out from the kitchen just in time to see them go. "Oh, no! The dish ran away with the spoon!" she shouted. "I borrowed those two artifacts from the library. What'll Ms. Goose say?" She actually looked a little nervous. Snow guessed that even the stern and scary Ms. Hagscorch worried about losing library artifacts or turning them in late.

The piping of faint musical notes drifted back to everyone in the Hall from outside as the pipe led the objects away. Principal R's eyes narrowed and his face went red. Standing on tiptoe, he hopped onto a chair and then onto one of the long tables. Then he reached out to Mr. Hump-Dumpty, who was standing nearby. After grabbing him by his jacket lapels, Principal R jerked him near. "Just look at the trouble you've caused!" he shouted.

Mr. Hump-Dumpty's huge egg-shaped eyes grew even bigger. "That pipe's not mine. I don't know where it came from. It — it just turned up," he stuttered.

"Oh, really?" Principal R said, dropping the egg-teacher's lapels and rocking back onto his heels. "Your brains must be scrambled if you think I'll believe that. Because a student saw it in your classroom just this morning!"

Snow froze. Principal R hadn't named her as the student, but would Mr. Hump-Dumpty guess it was her? She ducked when he glanced around at the crowd. His eyes seemed to linger on Wolfgang, who was among the group of students watching. There was a piteous expression on the egg-teacher's face, like he was hoping someone would come to his rescue. Only no one did. Nervously fingering the collar of his shirt he turned back to Principal R. "I'm telling you the truth. I'm not a bad egg. I don't know why, but someone planted that pipe in my classroom."

The principal's eyes bulged. As often happened when he became enraged, he began to hop up and down like a cricket. "Are you saying you've been framed?" he roared, almost slipping off the table. "Now *that* sounds like a real fairy tale!"

Just then, Snow caught a glimpse of Ms. Wicked through the crowd. She was standing to one side of the table with a smirk on her face. *She's enjoying this!* Snow realized with a shock. Then an idea hit her. The Scrying classroom was right next door to Mr. Hump-Dumpty's. Ms. Wicked could've easily taken the pipe from the library and planted it in the pocket of his jacket, which he often left hanging over the back of his chair. The question was, why would she do that to poor Mr. Hump-Dumpty?

6

Hunter

Snow glanced at Red and saw that she was studying Ms. Wicked, too. Then Red's eyes swung to Snow. They were filled with suspicion once again. Quickly, both girls looked away. The next time Snow searched the crowd for Red, she was gone.

Bongs echoed throughout the Hall, signaling the beginning of fifth period. Suddenly, Principal R seemed to notice the students standing all around him. "Shoo," he told them. "Get to your classes." Then, glaring at Mr. Hump-Dumpty, he said, "I'll see you in my office just as soon as school is out."

Snow and Cinda gave each other helpless looks as they separated to go to their respective classrooms. Snow was starting to have second thoughts about what they'd done. From the look on Cinda's face, she was, too. What if Mr. Hump-Dumpty really had been framed?

Snow was halfway to fifth-period Calligraphy and Illuminated Manuscripts class when she tripped again.

Frustrated, she stopped and frowned down at her feet. Just then, it flashed through her mind that there might be a connection between the tripping episodes that had happened since History class and her new shoelaces. What was it her stepmom had said before she'd handed them to Snow?

They'll work like magic.

Ha! She wouldn't be surprised if they really were magic and could tie and untie themselves at will. Because now that she thought about it, it had felt like her shoes were loosening and tightening in dance class each time she fell. They'd probably tied themselves together to make her trip, then quickly retied themselves normally so she wouldn't notice. *Nice gift, Stepmom. Not!*

Just in case she was right about the laces, Snow reached into her sparkly blue schoolbag for her old ones, which she hadn't yet tossed. Oddly, the old laces seemed to leap into her hand as soon as she opened her bag. She didn't even have to search for them! Odder still, the broken lace had been neatly mended. The dwarves must have done that when they'd swapped out her laces during History class. Talk about helpful! She closed her bag, sat on the stairs, and quickly swapped out the laces again.

As she entered her fifth-period classroom, she tossed the blue laces her stepmom had given her into the trash can just inside the door. Then she headed for her desk.

Sir Peter Pen, the Calligraphy and Illuminated Manuscripts instructor, was having all his classes make decorative place cards to be set on the tables at the upcoming ball. Although it had only been announced that morning, by now students had already nicknamed the ball *The Prince Prance*.

Pushing all thoughts about the treacherous laces — and her even more treacherous stepmom — out of her mind, Snow threw herself into the assignment. She loved forming words and numbers with the elegant black pen-strokes their teacher had taught them.

Forgetting for the moment that they weren't getting along all that well, Snow smiled at Red, who was also in this class. "Isn't this fun?" she enthused as she started on her third place card.

"It might be if I were any good at it," groused Red. She'd already crumpled and discarded two place cards. She'd spilled ink on one of them. The other had been illegible, with poorly formed letters as well as smudges.

"Oh, well," Snow said kindly. "Your talents lie elsewhere." In Drama is what she'd meant, but Red grinned. "Yes, *elsewhere*. As in, far outside this room."

They laughed together and Snow felt happy for a moment. Would it last?

After class, the two of them headed downstairs. Snow's footsteps dragged as she and Red made their way from the third floor to the first. She absolutely dreaded sixth period. She had Scrying class. With her stepmom. *Bleah.* It might have been easier if one of her BFF's was in class with her. No such luck.

The minute Snow entered the Scrying room, she noticed something was different. Usually, Ms. Wicked pounced on her right away with some criticism about her dress, her grooming, or even her manners. But today — nothing. Her stepmom didn't even seem to notice her arrival. Instead, she was huddled at her desk with Cinda's step-sisters, Malorette and Odette, who also took Scrying this period. The three of them were as thick as thieves, talking and gesturing animatedly. Those two snotty girls were pretty much teacher's pets in this class.

Like the other students, Snow grabbed a crystal ball from the shelf where they were stored. Before she could head for her seat, Ms. Wicked broke off from her conversation with Malorette and Odette. "Put away the crystal balls, students," she instructed everyone. "Today, we'll be using mirrors to look into the future."

Most everyone squeaked with delight at the news, but Snow shuddered as she did an about-face to return her ball to its shelf. Mirrors weirded her out. Especially the talking variety, like the one in the library that GA girls used to design new ball gowns.

Thonk! Snow put the crystal ball back on its shelf. Then she went to grab one of the small square mirrors hanging from little silver nails in rows on the far wall.

She took the long way, so she'd pass near Ms. Wicked's desk. Her footsteps slowed as she went by, and she strained to hear what her stepmom and Cinda's Steps were saying to one another. But she could only pick out a couple of words like "payback" and "good riddance to bad eggs."

They must be talking about Mr. Hump-Dumpty, she realized. It sounded as if they thought he was guilty of stealing the pipe and hoped he'd be fired.

Back at her desk, Snow set the mirror she'd gotten facedown. It was about the size of a playing card.

"Um, I think it goes the other way," said Hunter, the prince who sat to her left at the square table. He reached over and flipped her mirror reflective side up.

"Oh, thanks," she told him. She gave him a wide-eyed look. "I've never used a mirror before, so I didn't know." When he laughed at her joke, she did, too.

But when she stared down into her mirror, she saw the puzzlement in her face. She and her BFFs knew for sure that Malorette, Odette, and Ms. Wicked were all members of E.V.I.L. If they were rejoicing that Mr. Hump-Dumpty was in trouble, then he couldn't be a member of E.V.I.L., too, could he? Her spirits lifted at this deduction.

Suddenly, even though she hadn't asked it anything yet, the fuzzy outlines of a face appeared in the middle of the mirror Snow held. Becoming three-dimensional, the gleaming silver face pushed itself halfway out of the mirror.

Startled, she nearly dropped it as it began to speak:

"Ms. Wicked won't like what I've seen.
For you are fairer than the queen.
About her looks she is quite vain.
So she will cause you lots of pain."

What? thought Snow. The mirror seemed to be saying that she was *prettier* than her stepmom. That was crazy. Ms. Wicked was stunningly beautiful!

She glanced around at the students closest to her. By now, everyone else was intent on a conversation with their own mirror. Since no one was paying attention to her mirror, they hadn't heard what it said.

She stared down at it again. This mirror had been right about one thing — her stepmom *was* rather vain about her looks. Mirrors had been in every room of the castle when Snow was a child. Including the full-length one that was hanging on the wall at the front of this very classroom. Her stepmom now used the mirror to write assignments on — in red lipstick, no less! — instead of a whiteboard.

But if by "fairer," the little mirror on Snow's desk had only meant that she was more *fair-minded* than her step-mom, then that was true. As for Ms. Wicked causing her pain, that happened every day, so it was hardly news.

Snow let out a puff of air, blowing her bangs upward. "Tell me something I don't know," she told the mirror.

"Okay," it replied.

"No. Wait. I didn't mean —" Snow started to say. But the mirror had already begun to speak again:

"This Saturday there shall be a ball.
With dancing in the Academy's Hall."

Snow rolled her eyes. "That's not news, either," she said. Maybe her mirror was defective!

The face inside it frowned. "Ex-*CUSE* me. I wasn't finished," it said.

"Oh. Sorry," Snow said quickly. Even if it was just a mirror, she could still show it good manners. "Please continue," she said politely.

The mirror gave a haughty sniff, then went on:

"This may come as a giant blow.
But to the ball you will not go."

"What?" Snow exclaimed aloud. "Of course I'm going!"

She'd spoken loudly enough that Hunter looked up at her in surprise. Luckily, the room was so noisy with students and mirrors alike chattering away that no one else seemed to have noticed her outburst.

Snow bent over her mirror. "You're kidding, right?" she whispered to it. "I'm going to the ball. Why wouldn't I?"

But the mirror didn't reply. Its face had begun to slowly sink in upon itself, so it looked sort of like a balloon deflating.

"Wait!" she demanded. "Don't go!" But the mirror had already gone flat again.

"What's wrong? Malfunctioning mirror?" asked Hunter.

"You can say that again," she told him.

Hunter grinned. "What's wrong? Malfunctioning mirror?"

She managed a slight grin, but she was too annoyed at the mirror to laugh. That thing was defective for sure. She tilted the flat silver mirror a little, enough to see in its reflection that Malorette and Odette were in their seats now. Then she tilted it in a different direction and found her stepmom, who was standing several tables behind her. Ms. Wicked was slowly heading Snow's way as she checked on each student's work.

Writing her mirror's predictions was part of the class assignment, so Snow opened her bag to take out a sheet of vellum paper and an ink-filled quill pen. As had happened with the laces, the things she needed practically jumped into her hand as soon as she reached into her bag.

But she barely noticed because she was thinking hard now. She couldn't write what the mirror had told her. It would upset her stepmom and make trouble. *Besides, that mirror* had *to be wrong,* she thought as her pen tapped the paper. She *wasn't* more beautiful than Ms. Wicked. And of course she would go to the ball. Of all the balls she'd ever attended, this one was the most important to her. She wanted to be there to dance with Prince!

Snow hadn't been paying attention to what she was doing, so she was surprised when she glanced down after a bit at the vellum sheet and saw that she'd been doodling. And what she'd drawn was pretty embarrassing: a little heart with *Snow + Prince* written inside it!

She couldn't let her stepmom see that. It would lead to a million nosy questions. As she reached to crumple up the paper, however, she accidentally knocked it off her desk. It floated to the floor. Before she could retrieve it, Hunter picked it up. Annoyingly, instead of handing it back to her, he kept it to study.

"Give it back, Hunter," Snow commanded in a low voice only he would hear. Although he was kind-hearted, he was a cutup and had been known to lead many a student into trouble without meaning to. And she didn't need any more trouble right now.

But the curly-headed boy only held the paper over his head instead, so she couldn't reach it. "Looks like someone's crushing," he teased. "On Prince *who*, though? That's the question."

"Stop it," she pleaded. "I was just..." She glanced toward her stepmom worriedly. With the drawing still clenched in his upraised fist, Hunter followed her gaze.

Alerted by some sixth sense that always seemed to let her know when Snow was at her most vulnerable, Ms. Wicked frowned over at her.

"Uh-oh," said Hunter. His arm dropped as the teacher headed their way. Turning his back on her, he crumpled Snow's doodle and quickly stuffed it into his jacket pocket.

Ms. Wicked glared at her before giving Hunter one of her fake smiles. "May I see the note, please?" She stretched out her hand palm up.

Snow held her breath as she waited to see what Hunter would do.

"Note?" he asked innocently.

Her stepmom continued to smile at him, but through clenched teeth. "Yes. The one I saw you waving around. The one in your pocket."

"Oh, *that* note," Hunter said. He reached into his pocket and drew out a crumpled vellum sheet. "Here you go," he said, handing it over.

As Ms. Wicked un-crumpled the drawing and stared at it, he flashed Snow a quick grin. But she was half-frozen in horror. Didn't this annoying boy get that this was no laughing matter? If her stepmom knew she was crushing on someone, she'd watch Snow like a hawk till she figured out who it was. Then she'd make sure to ruin everything. She'd make Prince think badly of her. Snow wasn't sure how she'd do it, she just knew she would!

"A sketch of a deer?" Ms. Wicked announced in surprise.

Huh? Snow glanced over at the drawing and saw that it was indeed a sketch of a deer. Hunter must have had the sketch in his pocket all along and substituted it for her doodle!

"Actually, it's a *hart*," Hunter explained. "Which is the same as a fully grown stag. It's what I saw in my mirror just now."

"It's awesome," Snow said with relief. "The antlers almost look real." This, in fact, was true. Until now, she hadn't known what a good artist Hunter was. She gazed at him in admiration. And with gratitude, too. He'd saved her life! Well, maybe not her life. But he'd certainly saved her from being humiliated.

"Humpf," muttered Ms. Wicked. "It's very nice. However, you can draw when you're in Sir Peter Pen's class, but *not* in here. Please *write* your findings instead. Now get back to work, you two!" Wadding up the hart sketch, she tossed it into a wastebasket and stalked away.

"Oh, no," Snow murmured in dismay. "Your drawing!"

"No worries," said Hunter, shrugging carelessly. "I could draw another one in two seconds if I wanted to." While Ms. Wicked's back was still turned, he fished Snow's crumpled heart doodle from his pocket and tossed it to her.

She caught it and quickly stashed it in her blue bag.

"Friends again?" he asked.

Snow smiled and sent him a little nod. "Friends. Just please don't almost get me into trouble again?"

"Deal," he agreed. However, as usual, there was a mischievous twinkle in his eye.

Luckily, Ms. Wicked was busy talking to a couple of students when the period ended. Otherwise, she probably would've found a way to detain Snow, like by asking her to collect all the mirrors, just so she could have more time to criticize her. Carefully avoiding her stepmother's notice, and holding tight to her four-leaf clover amulet, Snow sneaked out of class.

With her bag over her shoulder, she hurried outside the Academy and over the drawbridge to meet her friends as planned. They were there waiting for her by the swan boats docked along the Pink Castle side of the Once Upon River.

"Got the mapestry?" Rapunzel asked.

Snow's fingers tightened on her blue bag. Her barely begun invisible-thread mapestry was inside it along with her GA Handbook. But of course Rapunzel had been speaking to Red, since the real mapestry was in her care.

"Yup." Red nodded toward her basket. "Got it."

As the girls paddled the short distance to Maze Island, they waved to Mermily, Cinda's mermaid roommate, who was already out in the river swimming laps.

"What a crazy day!" Cinda said, gazing at Snow as she dipped her paddle. "With the pipe and Mr. Hump-Dumpty and all that." By now everyone in the whole school had heard about the pipe playing a game of follow-the-leader in the Great Hall.

Snow peered up at the sky. "I wonder where it ended up?"

"Not in the Nothingterror, I hope," said Red.

"But that's probably the plan," said Rapunzel, dipping her paddle in the river's sparkling blue water. "Assuming someone is controlling it somehow and collecting other magical artifacts with it."

"How many artifacts do you think it'll take to destroy the wall that protects Grimmlandia?" asked Cinda.

Snow gulped. "No clue. But I've wondered the same thing." According to Grandmother Enchantress, the most famous and *ancient* enchantress they knew of, the protective spells that kept Grimmlandia safe from the outside world were further weakened each time magical artifacts were spirited out beyond the wall. And if those spells ever got too weak, Grimmlandia would be swallowed up in that most horrible place ever: the Dark Nothingterror!

"I bet whoever's controlling the pipe knows," said Red. "When it has gathered enough artifacts, they'll probably call the pipe toward the wall. . . ." Her voice tapered off and an awful silence fell over the girls for the rest of the trip.

Once they landed, their spirits picked up as they threaded their way through the pretty green hedge maze for which the island was named. It was mostly taller than they were, but parts were a little lopsided at the moment because they'd recently been replanted after Principal R's last alchemy disaster. Jack and Jill's pail had succeeded in putting that fire out, but the pail had disappeared shortly afterward. Again, Snow wondered about the fact that the pumpkin, the pail, and now the pipe were artifacts that all began with the letter *P*. If only they knew what it all meant!

At the center of the maze, the girls came upon a brand-new gazebo, which looked like a giant dome-like birdcage. It had been erected around a bronze statue of the Rumpster himself after the recent fire. Having seen no one else on the island, the girls entered it. Inside, Snow circled the life-size statue, noting the slightly melted places that had resulted from the alchemy accident in which the principal and Ms. Jabberwocky had unsuccessfully tried to turn it to gold.

"Is Grandmother Enchantress's crystal ball in a safe place?" she suddenly thought to ask Red. That ball was a very valuable object — way more powerful than the ones students practiced on in her stepmom's Scrying classes.

"Wolfgang hid it," said Red, after a slight hesitation. Snow had the impression she was choosing her words carefully, like she was afraid of revealing too much. Snow stared hard at her, but Red avoided her eyes and went to sit on one of the benches that encircled the inside of the gazebo. Snow's heart sank and wild thoughts flew through her mind. Something was definitely up. Was this more than just suspicion? Was Red planning to totally ditch her as a friend? How did the others feel about her?

Not long ago, it had been Wolfgang that all four girls mistrusted. They'd thought he might be a member of E.V.I.L., along with Snow's stepmom and Cinda's two step-sisters. After all, he'd stolen Red's basket while they were out in the woods searching for the Enchantress's cottage. And he'd even disguised himself as the enchantress and fooled Red into telling him things about the treasure they were hoping to find.

Afterward, Red had told them that Wolfgang had had good reasons for what he'd done, and that they could trust him. She hadn't revealed what those reasons were, and the other three girls hadn't pushed. They all knew that the enchantress, who they trusted implicitly, had tasked

Wolfgang with guarding her ball. Despite that, Snow still didn't totally trust the boy. And she couldn't help wondering if he'd said things to Red to fuel her mistrust of Snow.

As Red took the mapestry out of her basket and unrolled it, the others joined her on the benches. Together they studied the golden stitches that would lead them to where the mapestry wanted them to go. Just days before, a different trail of golden stitches had led them to the enchantress's cottage — and her crystal ball — at the center of Neverwood Forest. But afterward, those stitches had disappeared. As these new ones would, too, once the girls had found whatever it was they were supposed to find next.

Red ran a finger over the golden stitches, which now led from the forest back to the Academy to end in a large cross-stitch *X* at the very center of Pink Castle. Did that mean the treasure the girls hoped to find — one big enough to fix the Academy's troubled finances — had been right under their noses the whole time?

"So tonight's the night. The treasure hunt," said Rapunzel. When the others nodded, she added, "It's going to be hard searching inside the castle. We'll have to be extra careful not to let anyone figure out what we're doing." Then she shot a glance at the statue of Principal R. "It's weird talking about all this in front of him, even if he is only a statue!" she whispered.

Cinda giggled. "I know! I was just thinking the same thing."

Red nodded. Then she hopped up and threw off her red cape, draping it over the statue's head. "You never know," she said as she sat down again. "E.V.I.L. could have eyes everywhere."

It seemed to Snow that Red stared directly at her as she said this. Maybe now was the time to show her friends the fake mapestry. It might help Red trust her more. She lifted her bag into her lap, then hesitated. They wouldn't be able to see her stitches till it was finished. So they might not believe her. She pulled the fake mapestry out anyway and began stitching where she'd left off. Because the sooner she finished it the better!

"Secret project?" Red asked, noticing she was using invisible thread.

"Just Threads homework. I picked up the wrong kind of thread by accident," Snow replied, with a casual shrug. Luckily, Red didn't seem to think a simple stitching project warranted more suspicion.

"Wouldn't it be grimmsolutely *grimmazing* if we did find the treasure this time?" said Rapunzel, drawing their attention. Then she sighed. "But it's just as possible we'll find another magical object instead."

"If so, I hope it's Jack and Jill's pail," said Cinda. "I worry that it's already gone over the wall like Peter Peter's pumpkin."

"I worry about that, too," said Snow as she poked her needle in and out. "If the pipe leads even more artifacts over the wall, Grimmlandia could soon be toast." They had to get those artifacts back before it was too late! "So what time do we start the hunt?" she asked, looking up from her stitching.

"Midnight? After everyone is asleep?" suggested Red, going over to the statue to get her hooded cape back. "If we divide up, each taking a floor to search, we can cover more ground."

"Ooh! Too creepy. I think we should stick together," said Cinda. "At least our first time hunting. We could all meet on the second floor landing to begin."

Rapunzel and Red nodded. "Works for me," added Snow, putting her work away. She'd tackle the fake mapestry again before bed.

"Here's hoping we discover treasure!" said Cinda. She raised her hand in the air, waiting. One by one, the other three girls raised theirs for a joint high five, or actually a high *four*, if you were counting *hands*.

As they rowed back toward the Academy, Cinda suddenly said, "We forgot to talk about Saturday's Prince Prance! We need to meet at the library soon to reserve our ball gowns and slippers, like we did for Prince Awesome's ball."

74

"Let's do it tomorrow night," Rapunzel suggested, dipping her paddle on the other side of the boat.

Red shook her head. "Can't. I've got play practice Thursday."

"Friday, then?" said Rapunzel as their boat touched shore. "After dinner?"

"Sounds good," said Cinda. She hopped out and tugged them up onto the pebbly beach. Then the other three climbed out, too.

"Um . . . sure," Snow said belatedly as the Scrying mirror's prediction flitted through her mind. But the mirror had been wrong. She *would* go to that dance!

7

Midnight Madness

"Psst! Snow, it's time to go."

"Huh?" Snow woke with a start. In the dark she could barely see Cinda, except for her candle-flame yellow hair, which stood out even in the near pitch-black. She was standing on the ladder at the end of Snow's high canopy bed, tugging on her covers. From across the room in an identical bed came the soft, steady breathing of Snow's slumbering roommate, Jill.

Oh, no! Snow shoved her blue schoolbag deep under her covers. She'd brought it up here planning to work on the fake mapestry. But instead, she'd fallen asleep! She'd have to work extra hard in Threads class tomorrow and spend tomorrow night working on her secret project, too, if she hoped to finish it soon.

Careful not to wake her roommate, Snow followed Cinda down the ladder. "I'm going to change out of my pj's. See you in a few," Cinda whispered when she reached the floor. She disappeared through the curtain that served as a door to Snow and Jill's small alcove, and headed off to her own room.

Since she hadn't planned on falling asleep, Snow was still wearing the same gown she'd worn all day long. She smoothed the wrinkles from her skirt — Ms. Wicked hated wrinkles. Then she grabbed a brush from the top of her desk and brushed her hair without using a mirror, as always.

As she brushed, Snow's gaze fell on the framed, embroidered *Luck Comes to Those Who Are Prepared* sign that hung on her armoire. In the dim moonlight falling through the window, she could just make out the beautifully stitched border of four-leaf clovers that surrounded the words.

Noticing that the sign was hanging a bit crooked, Snow lifted it from its hook. Before she could re-hang it, it slipped from her fingers and nearly dropped. She caught it just in time. *Phew*, she thought, as she rehung the sign nice and straight. Good thing she was wearing her lucky clover amulet. Automatically, she reached toward her throat to touch it, but her fingers only met with bare skin. Her necklace — and with it, her amulet and trunker key — were gone!

Her breath caught and her heart began to race. *Calm down*, she told herself. *Probably, it simply fell off in bed.* She rushed back up her ladder and carefully felt around in her bedcovers, but the only thing she came up with was her schoolbag.

The curtain slid back and Cinda popped her head around it. "Snow? You ready?" she whispered.

Quickly, Snow shoved her bag back under the covers. "In a minute," she said. She tried not to let her panic grow out of control. After all, her necklace must be somewhere inside the room. She didn't have time to look for it now, though. Besides, it was too dark to see without lighting a lamp, which could wake Jill. She'd have to wait till morning.

After climbing back down from her bed, she rummaged around on a shelf at the top of her armoire. She kept some of her favorite lucky items and bad luck protections there, including a shiny agate she'd found by the river one day, a peacock feather, a brass button of her dad's, and a salt shaker in the shape of a ladybug. *Does Prince know that ladybugs are lucky if they land on you?* she wondered. She'd have to tell him sometime. Maybe he'd have some luck tips to share with her, too!

Being careful not to drop the shaker as she lifted it from the shelf — accidentally spilling salt was unlucky — Snow sprinkled a few grains into the palm of her hand. Then she tossed the salt over her left shoulder. *There!* That should help keep bad luck at bay while she and her friends were searching for treasure tonight. But just in case that wasn't enough, Snow also tucked the shiny agate into the pocket of her gown.

Moments later, she met Cinda, who wore her glass slippers, and Red, who carried her basket, in the dorm common room. "I'm hoping my magic slippers will help lead us to the treasure," Cinda explained as they crept down the twisty tower stairs. "Just like they led me to where the mapestry was hidden under that floor tile in the Great Hall."

As soon as she said this, her slippers did a little tap dance on the very step she was standing on. Cinda stared down at them. "Yes, you can help us," she said. "But just walk for now. Okay?" The slippers stopped tap dancing, appearing to understand.

The stairs eventually took them lower to the grand staircase, where they met Rapunzel. They were all about to push through the stairwell door on the second floor, when they heard footsteps coming down the steps behind them. They also heard the thump of a walking stick, followed by the sound of two grown-ups talking.

Snow's heart leaped into her throat and her eyes flew wide. "My stepmom's coming down the stairs," she announced in a shocked whisper.

"And Mr. Hump-Dumpty," added Red.

"What are they doing up this late?" hissed Rapunzel.

"C'mon. Hurry!" whispered Cinda.

The girls opened the stairwell door as quietly as they could and piled out into the second-floor hall. Leaving the door open just a crack, they hid behind it, hoping to hear

what the teachers said to each other on their way downstairs. Snow reached in her pocket and grasped her lucky
agate, willing it to protect the girls from discovery.

Click. Click.

Step. Thump. Step.

"It's simple," Ms. Wicked was saying as she came down
the steps. "You give me back the diary, and I'll tell R that I
saw one of the *students* put the Pied Piper of Hamelin's pipe
in your office."

"She calls the principal *R*," Snow whispered when she
saw Cinda looked confused. It sounded like her stepmom
was offering to lie in order to make some kind of deal with
Mr. Hump-Dumpty in exchange for a diary. But whose
diary? Ms. Wicked's? Did she even keep a diary? Snow had
never seen her stepmom write in one, but if she did it would
be like her to be secretive about it. And how would Mr.
Hump-Dumpty have gotten hold of it, anyway?

"Just pipe down about that pipe, can't you? If we do
nothing, the whole incident will blow over eventually," Mr.
Hump-Dumpty replied in a worried tone.

"Look," Ms. Wicked interrupted, in an exasperated
voice Snow knew only too well. "I'll even say that *Snow*
stole the pipe if you'd like me to. Whatever it takes to get
that diary from you. So how about it?"

Snow had to cover her mouth to stop herself from gasp-
ing aloud. Her stepmom's lowest low had just gone even

lower. She felt Cinda's arm wrap around her shoulders. Someone touched her arm — Red. And Rapunzel rested her hand on Snow's back, as all three friends offered comfort.

Click. Click. Step. Thump. Step.

"You'd throw your own daughter to the wolves?" Mr. Hump-Dumpty said disdainfully. His voice was louder now as the teachers reached the second floor landing.

"*Step*daughter," Ms. Wicked corrected him. "And from what you've told me about her finding the pipe in your classroom this morning, I suspect she was the one who reported you to R. You do know that, don't you?"

"Even if she did that still doesn't make it right to — hold on," he said, interrupting himself. "I need to rest a minute and catch my breath."

Snow could hear him huffing and puffing as the two grown-ups stopped on the stairs right by the door the girls crouched behind. Holding her breath, Snow squeezed her lucky agate even harder. *Please don't let them find us,* she wished silently.

"Speaking of wolves," Ms. Wicked said slyly. "I could pin the theft on Wolfgang if you'd rather. He's the one who stole the pipe in the first place."

"What?" Mr. Hump-Dumpty said in surprise.

"I'm sure Ell would be willing to sacrifice one measly wolf-boy for the sake of E.V.I.L.'s higher purpose."

Snow turned her head to stare at Red. Red had assured them that Wolfgang wasn't a member of E.V.I.L. Had he been lying to her? To all of them, in effect?

Suddenly, Snow remembered seeing Wolfgang race out of Mr. Hump-Dumpty's room just before she entered it that morning. Had he stolen the pipe, dropped it off in History class, and then gone into Scrying to report his actions to her stepmom? It would've been hard to sneak the pipe into Mr. Hump-Dumpty's jacket while he was wearing it and with lots of students in the room. However, Wolfgang was a sneaky one.

But what was this about a higher purpose? And who was *Ell*? And what did that diary have to do with anything?

"This whole matter stinks like a rotten *deviled* egg," muttered Mr. Hump-Dumpty. "All right, I'm keeping the diary for further examination, but I'll give you what you want from it."

"Deal," said Ms. Wicked. The two teachers continued down the stairs. *Click. Click. Step. Thump. Step.*

Though deeply confused, Snow breathed a sigh of relief and silently thanked her lucky agate for sending them away.

"If Wolfgang did steal that pipe, I'm positive he did it for a very good reason," Red whispered to the other girls as they continued to huddle together.

Snow couldn't believe Red was defending him! "I'm pretty sure he did plant that pipe on Mr. Hump-Dumpty," she argued. "I even saw him leaving History class just before third period started."

"Does he have History second period?" Cinda asked Red.

"Well, no, but —"

"So Wolfgang had no reason to be there!" said Snow. She and Red jumped up and faced off.

"Shh, you guys!" Rapunzel hissed.

"There's stuff you don't know," Red said in a quieter voice. Something shifted in her eyes, and once again, Snow got the feeling that Red mistrusted her. Disheartened, she started to reach for the door to the second-floor hall, but Rapunzel stopped her.

Nodding downstairs to where the two teachers had gone, she said, "Don't open the door yet. It squeaks, and they might hear it."

"Yeah, and don't talk so loud," said Cinda, looking between Red and Snow.

"If Wolfgang did plant that pipe, it was on your step-mom's orders," Red told Snow in a calmer voice. Then, as if she couldn't help herself, she added, "He's on our side. He's been trying to get into E.V.I.L. so that he can *spy* on them."

All three girls gasped, but Red didn't wait for questions. "To join the Society, he had to steal something magically important for his initiation. So I let him give Ms. Wicked my basket. But then I called it back to me right away, so I guess she made Wolfgang get something else."

"The pipe!" exclaimed Cinda, slowly getting to her feet.

Red nodded. "But Wolfgang wouldn't have planted the pipe on Mr. Hump-Dumpty. He just *wouldn't.* Even on Ms. Wicked's orders."

"You should've told us," said Rapunzel.

Snow gulped at that, knowing that she was keeping secrets, too, about that crystal ball order form and her fake mapestry. But she couldn't still her doubts about Wolfgang. "He might be tricking you," she told Red. "Tricking *all* of us."

"He isn't," Red insisted. Her eyes flashed at Rapunzel and Snow, and Snow looked away, wishing she'd kept quiet.

"Stop that!" scolded Cinda, causing everyone to glance at her in surprise. But she was gazing down, speaking to her glass slippers. Because they'd begun to tap dance again, as if anxious to be moving on. As she stood in place they whirled her in a circle.

Creak! A door slammed shut one floor below. "That must be the first-floor door," Snow murmured.

"Sounded like it," Rapunzel agreed. "It also sounds like Ms. Wicked is trying to *blackmail* Mr. Hump-Dumpty over a diary!"

Red nodded in agreement. "Only, why? I mean, they must both be members of the Society or else Ms. Wicked wouldn't have mentioned E.V.I.L. to him just now."

"Maybe he's having some second thoughts about being in E.V.I.L.," Rapunzel suggested. "Maybe he wants out."

Bang! Bang! Unable to contain themselves any longer, Cinda's slippers had begun to kick at the stairwell door. "Sorry," she told the others. "I can't control them when they want to get moving. Maybe they're trying to tell us something."

Rapunzel pushed open the door to the stairwell and peered downward. "Let's see where they lead us."

"Wait. We don't want to go down to the first floor," said Red. "That's where Ms. Wicked and Mr. Hump-Dumpty went. Besides, we were going to search this one first."

Too late. Because the minute the door opened, Cinda's slippers were off and dancing!

"Whoa!" she hissed at them. "Hold your horses!" But the slippers didn't pause. They tap-danced their way down the stairs, taking Cinda along for the ride. The other three girls followed on her heels. At the first floor landing, the slippers kicked at the door which led down the hall to the first-floor classrooms. *Bang! Bang! Bang!*

"Stop!" Cinda scolded them in alarm. But the slippers wouldn't obey.

"Shh! I hear something!" hissed Rapunzel. Meanwhile, Cinda stooped and pulled the slippers off her feet.

"Someone's coming!" Red warned.

Click. Click. Step. Thump. Step.

Alerted by the kicks on the first-floor door, it sounded like Ms. Wicked and Mr. Hump-Dumpty were heading back toward it. It was against school rules to be running around in the halls this late. *They'd probably get double triple demerits!* thought Snow. Which would mean they couldn't go to the ball on Saturday. Was that crazy, probably defective, Scrying mirror's prediction about to come true after all?

8

The Dungeon

"Quick!" Rapunzel told the three girls. "Follow me!"

She continued down the stairs, and the others scurried after her. When they reached the basement landing, Rapunzel fished out a key, thrust it into a lock, and then threw open a narrow black door with big iron hinges. After they went through, she locked it behind them. The door led them into a long, sloping tunnel paved with cobblestones. Antique brass lamps stuck out from the tunnel walls every few feet to light their way.

Together they ventured deep below the castle, heading for Rapunzel's room. She'd gotten special permission from Principal R to bunk down here in the dungeon. In Snow's opinion that proved she'd do anything to avoid having to climb to the highest turrets of the Pink Castle dorms. Because this dungeon was really creepy! The girls hadn't gone more than two dozen steps down the tunnel when Cinda gasped.

"What's the matter?" Red asked anxiously as all four girls came to a halt. "Stub your toe on a cobblestone?"

"No, I was in such a hurry to get away before Ms. Wicked and Mr. Hump-Dumpty caught us that I didn't stop to put my slippers back on." The girls glanced down to see that Cinda was in fact walking in her stocking feet. She held up a single glass slipper. "And I just realized I must've dropped my other slipper back there somewhere. I don't know why I have such trouble holding on to both slippers. It's just like after Prince Awesome's ball."

She'd dropped one then, too. Understandable, though. She'd been in a hurry to get away from the ball. Because her gown had begun shooting off fireworks! She hadn't gone back for the slipper, but Prince Awesome had returned it to her later in a sweet scene that had made the girls who'd been there to witness it smile and sigh happily.

"I think I lost it before we came in here, which means it's still outside the tunnel. If those teachers see it, we'll be caught!" Cinda turned and raced back up the tunnel, going after her slipper.

"I'll help you look for it," said Rapunzel.

"Wait!" Snow called to them just as they reached the tunnel door and were about to turn the knob. She looked at Red. "Use your basket!"

"Hurry! I hear footsteps coming," whispered Cinda, hopping from one foot to the other. Sure enough, there were sounds on the basement landing right outside the narrow black door. *Click. Click. Step. Thump. Step.*

"A tisket, a tasket," Red said in a rush. "Fetch Cinda's missing glass slipper, basket!"

Heart pounding, Snow counted the words after *tasket* on her fingers. Good, there were six of them — the required number for the basket to work its magic properly.

Red lifted the hinged lid of her basket. "Got it!" she said, handing the missing slipper to Cinda. Just then someone rattled the knob of the narrow tunnel door. Cinda jumped back, staring at it in horror. She and Rapunzel turned and zoomed back to join Snow and Red.

"It's locked," the girls heard Mr. Hump-Dumpty say.

"No problem. My handbag can always find a key," Ms. Wicked replied in a sly voice.

"She can conjure just about anything she wants out of that purse," Snow warned the others in a whisper.

"Aha! Here we go," said Ms. Wicked. A key rattled in the lock.

The girls froze in place, holding their breath. Snow reached into her pocket for her lucky agate. It was gone! Too late, her fingers discovered the hole in her pocket. Her stomach plunged down to her toes. Without a lucky charm, she felt like a knight without his armor. A book without a cover. A turtle without its shell. Basically, she figured they were doomed!

Just then, Red whispered something to her basket. Rapunzel elbowed her and put a finger to her lips.

"The key!" they heard Ms. Wicked say. "It disappeared from my hand!"

Now it was Red's turn to nudge the other girls. She opened her basket's lid wide enough for them to see inside it. She'd gotten the key! That's why she'd been whispering a moment ago. She'd been giving her basket instructions to nab it.

Ms. Wicked conjured a second key and tried again, but Red used her basket to take that one, too. After Ms. Wicked lost a third key, Mr. Hump-Dumpty spoke up. "I'm heading back upstairs. It's too damp down here for an egg like me," he said. "Besides, I gave you the page you wanted. Let's go."

The *page* she wanted? *What was that all about?* Snow wondered.

Ms. Wicked let out a frustrated sigh. Then she raised her voice slightly as if she'd somehow sensed that the girls were listening. "Whoever we heard had better take care with what they know. Because students who disobey school rules don't fare well."

Click. Click. Step. Thump. Step. As the pair left, the girls all looked at one another with wide eyes. They began backing down the tunnel. Then they turned and dashed all the rest of the way to Rapunzel's room.

"Do you think she guessed it was us?" whispered Cinda breathlessly as they reached the heavy iron door that led into the room. The door had a barred window in it since, creepily enough, the room had been used as a prison cell at one time.

"She can't prove it," said Snow, trying to sound braver than she felt. After all, it was common knowledge that Rapunzel roomed in the dungeon. And her stepmom knew that Rapunzel was one of Snow's BFFs.

We're safe for now, though, thought Snow as the girls all pushed through the door. *Phew!* Somehow, even without the help of a lucky clover or agate, she and her friends had lucked out. Then again, maybe the salt she'd thrown over her shoulder before she'd left her room was what had kept them safe. That, and Red thinking to use her basket to snatch those keys, of course!

As soon as the girls entered the room, three of Rapunzel's cats — she had five of them — padded over and began to rub up against everyone's legs.

Luckily, Snow wasn't allergic to animal fur, just fruit. She reached down to pet Shadow, a gray cat that was super soft and fluffy, as Rapunzel hurried to light a small oil lamp. Once the lamp blazed to life, Snow straightened and glanced around to see if Rapunzel had made any changes to her room lately.

For a dungeon room, it was really cute — in a goth kind of way. Black lacy curtains hung from a second barred window at the far end. Below the window sat Rapunzel's bed. The thick goose-down comforter on top of it was covered in a black duvet. Raven and Midnight, two practically identical black cats, were curled up together in the middle of it.

A black-and-white checkered rug lay on the floor beside the bed, and across from that were a black-painted desk and an armoire. Tasseled black-and-white pillows of various shapes and sizes were scattered about the room. But the most awesome thing was what Rapunzel had done with the cold, stone walls.

"Those murals are grimmcredible!" Cinda declared as Mordred, a black cat with a white star on his forehead, threaded between her legs. Since she'd only started at the Academy recently, she'd never been down to the dungeon before, Snow realized. Cinda turned toward Rapunzel. "Did you paint them yourself?"

Rapunzel nodded, flashing Cinda a pleased smile as she scooped up Moon, her only white cat.

The murals really were grimmcredible. Painted in various shades of black, silver, white, and other dusky colors, they showed a forest scene at night. As bats and owls flitted through a moonlit sky, heavy-limbed trees swayed below them.

Snow sat on the edge of Rapunzel's bed, sinking into the thick comforter. Stretching, Midnight unwound himself and came to snuggle in her lap. The other three girls grabbed pillows and sat on the rug.

"So much for treasure-hunting," said Cinda. Yawning, she flopped onto her back.

"Too true. That was kind of a bust," agreed Rapunzel.

"Maybe. Maybe not," said Red. She set her basket in her lap and tossed the keys she'd taken from Ms. Wicked to Rapunzel, who took them and tossed them over to her desk. Then she gave Cinda the glass slipper she'd lost. As Cinda slipped on both shoes, Red pulled out the mapestry and unrolled it on the rug. Immediately, Mordred slinked over and lay on top of it before she could study it. She left him there for now, petting him.

"I can't believe your stepmom was willing to lie and say that *you'd* stolen the pipe," Rapunzel said to Snow.

"That's just the kind of evil thing my stepsisters would do to me," Cinda added.

"Yeah," Snow said softly. A lump rose in her throat as she ran her hand down Midnight's soft back. She would never, ever trust her stepmom again!

"She won't do it, though, right?" Red said uncertainly. "She'll pin the blame on Wolfgang instead?" She didn't sound very happy about either idea.

Snow raised and lowered her shoulders in an unsure way. "Guess we'll see."

Cinda sat up, her forehead furrowed in thought. "Let's try to figure this thing out. We know Grandmother Enchantress is working to stop E.V.I.L.," she said slowly. "And from what we overheard on the stairs just now, it doesn't sound like Principal R is a member of the Society. I wonder if he knows Wolfgang is helping the enchantress?"

"He *might*," Red said with a frown. "But how would that help Wolf —"

"I see where Cinda's going," interrupted Rapunzel as Moon jumped up to go chase a tassel that had moved on her cushion. "If Principal R knows, or finds out, that Wolfgang and the enchantress are working against E.V.I.L., then he won't punish Wolfgang, no matter what he's done."

So do Cinda and Rapunzel both buy Wolfgang's spy story? Snow wondered. *Looks like* I'm *the only one who has doubts about him!*

Cinda tilted her chin. "But Grumpystiltskin would *have* to do something if Ms. Wicked told him that Wolfgang stole the Pied Piper's pipe from the library, wouldn't he? Or else Ms. Wicked would suspect that both he and Wolfgang are working against the Society."

The girls all fell silent, thinking. Then Cinda yawned. "Well, it's really late."

Everyone nodded, all looking confused and a little disheartened. Rapunzel lifted Mordred off the mapestry and gave him a hug. As she set him aside, her eyes fell on the mapestry. "Too bad the stitchery of the castle isn't large enough or detailed enough to show which floor the *X* is on," she said.

At this, Cinda's slippers, which she'd taken off her feet and set on the floor beside her, began to fidget. Suddenly, they leaped from the floor onto Rapunzel's bed, scaring

Mordred so badly that, giving a yowl, he jumped down from the bed and hid under it. After tap, tap, tapping at the edges of the mapestry, the slippers then leaped to the floor again and raced to Rapunzel's door to kick at it. "Do you suppose they're trying to tell us something?" Cinda asked.

"Like maybe *they* know where we should be searching?" added Red.

Suddenly, they were all wide awake again.

"I say we follow Cinda's slippers and see where they want us to go!" Snow exclaimed.

After a chorus of "*me too*s," all four girls jumped to their feet and headed for the door. Rapunzel grabbed the oil lamp to take with them. "I'll be back soon," she assured her cats. Then she waited till the other three girls were out before shutting the door behind her.

Cinda had put on her glass slippers again, and they merrily danced her down the tunnel. The others hurried to keep up as they trailed her all the way through the tunnel door, then up a flight of stairs to the first-floor landing. There the slippers once more kicked at the door. Luckily, Ms. Wicked and Mr. Hump-Dumpty weren't around to hear them this time! Slipping through the first floor door, the girls followed as the glass slippers led them along the curved hallway.

It felt weirdly empty and eerie here this late at night, thought Snow. So quiet and still. And dark. She really hated to think about the grimmzillion demerits they'd get if they were caught. They'd already had *one* narrow escape!

Cinda's slippers danced their way to Mr. Hump-Dumpty's classroom. Then, without pause, they waltzed Cinda over to his desk. And there they stopped. "Here?" she asked them. They gave a little stamp as if to say *yes*, and then stood still again.

There was a book open on top of Mr. Hump-Dumpty's desk. The girls gathered around as Cinda picked it up. "Do you think this is what we're meant to find?"

Red took a quick look at the mapestry she held, then said in an excited voice, "Must be. The golden thread path is fading away."

Rapunzel held the lamp closer to the book. It had a cracked brown leather cover, and its yellowing pages were covered with elegant, flowing handwriting. "*Dear Diary*," she read aloud from the first page.

"This must be the diary Ms. Wicked and Mr. Hump-Dumpty were talking about!" declared Snow. She flipped through it. "It's not my stepmom's handwriting. Do you think it's Mr. Hump-Dumpty's?"

"It looks really old. Like it was written a long, *looong* time ago," said Rapunzel.

"And whoever wrote it must have gotten straight A's in Calligraphy and Illuminated Manuscripts," Red noted.

Cinda flipped through a few more pages as the other

girls looked on. The written entries told about classes at Grimm Academy and gave details about homework assignments and about students whose names the girls didn't recognize.

"Check inside the front cover for a name," Snow suggested.

Cinda flipped back to the beginning. "I found something! It says, *This diary is the property of Lotte G.*"

"Lotte G.?" Red repeated. "Does that name ring a bell for anyone?" The other three shrugged.

As Cinda began to flip through the book again, something caught Snow's eye. "Wait! Let me see that thing."

After Cinda handed her the book, Snow held it upside down, grasping the cover in either hand so that the pages fanned out as they dangled from the spine. Then she eyeballed the pages, looking for the slight gap she'd noticed only moments before. She flattened the book on the desktop again and pointed to a ragged tear inside the book that ran the length of the spine. "There's a page missing," she announced. "It's been torn out."

She looked up at the others. "Mr. Hump-Dumpty said my stepmom got *the page she wanted*, remember?"

"Yeah! So what was on that torn-out page?" Red asked. Her eyes went to Snow.

"Don't look at me," Snow said. "My stepmom doesn't tell me anything." She started to add, *And I don't tell her anything, either*. But just then the girls heard thumping sounds out in the hallway.

"Shh," cautioned Rapunzel. After turning down the lamp, she crept to the door and peeked out its small glass-pane window. "It's Wee Willie Winkie," she reported back. He was the night custodian, but he also kept an eye out for students wandering around past bedtime.

"Demerits, here we come," Snow groaned softly.

"Shh! Get down," said Cinda. They all dropped to a crouch behind the desk, just in case. As soon as Mr. Winkie pushed past Mr. Hump-Dumpty's room, sweeping the wide hall with his broom, the girls all breathed a sigh of relief.

Red frowned. "I bet there are clues in it leading to treasure. And now Ms. Wicked has them."

"Let's take the diary with us to study, though, just in case there are any other pages with clues she overlooked," Rapunzel suggested.

"But Mr. Hump-Dumpty will notice it's missing," Snow protested.

"Well, but it's not really *his*," Red pointed out. "It's Lotte G.'s."

"And my glass slippers led us right to it," added Cinda. "They and the mapestry wanted us to find it."

No one could argue with that logic, so Red slipped the diary into her basket for safekeeping. Then, before Wee Willie Winkie could round the circular hallway and come upon them as they made their escape, the girls crept out of the room, closing the door softly behind them.

Once out on the first floor landing again, Snow, Cinda, and Red said good-bye to Rapunzel and started back to their rooms on the sixth floor so they could get some sleep before Thursday's classes.

When Snow returned to her room, she put on her pajamas and took the ladder up to her bed. Yawning, she took her blue bag from under the bedcover and pulled the fake mapestry from it. Even though she was super tired, she was determined to get some more work done on it. Only when she looked down at it, she gasped. It was already half finished! The entire blue area of Once Upon River and most of Neverwood Forest were completed. Who could have done this?

She looked over at Jill in the bed across the room. No way. Her roommate didn't sleepwalk. And even if she did, she wouldn't have climbed up on Snow's bed, searched out her bag, and worked on a needlepoint project. Besides, the threads would be invisible to her! No. The only explanation that made any sense was that Snow had sewn it herself before Cinda had come to wake her at midnight. She must have been half-asleep while she sewed, and that's why she'd forgotten what she'd done. Yes. That had to be it.

9

Best and Brightest

In spite of her late night, Snow woke up early the next morning. She checked the fake mapestry again, first thing. No, she hadn't been dreaming. It *was* half finished. In fact, it was more than half finished. Had even more gotten done overnight? Weird! But Grimmlandia *was* a magical place. Maybe some random magic had done this for her. That was lucky!

Remembering that her clover necklace was missing, she tucked the mapestry back inside her blue bag with her GA Handbook, and then searched the whole room. When she didn't find it, she tried scouring the Pearl Tower common room. No luck.

"Try to remember when you last saw it," Cinda advised her at breakfast when Snow finally told her friends that her lucky necklace was missing. Then she yawned. They were all tired from last night.

Snow set down the hot cross bun she'd been nibbling on. "Well, I showed it to Prince after History class yesterday because I found out he has a lucky coin." She thought for a minute. "And I'm pretty sure I had it during Scrying class after that."

"I wish I could remember if you had it on while we were out on Maze Island," Rapunzel said. "But I can't." No one else could recall if Snow had had it on then, either.

Red's basket, which sat on the bench beside her, began to jiggle as if trying to get their attention. Her face lit up. "Maybe my basket can fetch it!"

"Oh, that would be so perfect!" Snow said in relief. "I can't believe I didn't think of asking you to try that last night." The offer made her extra happy because it meant Red must still be her friend if she was so willing to do this favor, right?

"A tisket, a tasket, please fetch Snow's clover necklace, basket," Red said. She waited a few seconds before eagerly pulling down on the basket's handles and opening its hinged lid.

Red looked in one side and Snow leaned over to look in the other side. The rolled-up mapestry was there. So was the diary the girls had taken from Mr. Hump-Dumpty's desk. Keeping the lid low so that no one nearby could catch sight of those things, Snow stuck a hand inside the basket and poked all around for her necklace. Eventually, she gave up, hugely disappointed. "It's not there."

The girls let go of both sides of the lid, which then flopped down. The basket hopped toward Snow and patted her arm with one of its handles as if to say sorry.

"That's okay. I know you tried," Snow told it.

Red was counting on her fingers and frowning. "I don't understand why that didn't work. I used six words to make my request."

Rapunzel's forehead wrinkled. "Maybe the necklace is someplace where the basket's magic is blocked."

"Like where?" asked Cinda. "Oh, wait! My stepsisters hid Peter Peter's pumpkin in my trunker to keep the library's magic from automatically returning the pumpkin to the library, remember?"

"So maybe my basket's magic can't fetch things under certain conditions," Red mused. Magical charms didn't come with a full set of instructions. You had to *discover* what they could do.

"Wait!" Snow said as a happy thought came to her. "Maybe someone already found my necklace and took it to the Lost and Found box in Ms. Jabberwocky's office. Your basket's magic probably couldn't fetch it from the box if that's where it is. I'll go check at lunch." She didn't dare be late to her classes this morning after being late yesterday.

"Don't forget that we're meeting after school in the library to examine the *D-Book*," Red reminded everyone in code before they split up to go to their classes.

During her second-period Threads class, Snow whipped through more of her fake mapestry, stitching an image of Gray Castle and part of Maze Island. She was surprised that her first two classes went as well as they did, especially since she'd been so upset about her missing necklace that she'd forgotten to throw salt over her shoulder to protect herself from bad luck that morning.

Nor had she remembered to take one of her other lucky charms with her. There wasn't enough time between classes to run back up to her dorm room to fetch one. Too bad she hadn't thought at breakfast to ask Red to see if her basket could fetch the lucky agate she'd lost from her pocket last night. She could ask at lunch, but that wouldn't help her right now.

Without her usual protections, Snow wasn't sure she'd be able to avoid her stepmom out in the hallway before her third-period History class. But somehow she did.

Mr. Hump-Dumpty was busily rummaging through the drawers of his desk at the front of the room as Snow took her seat. *Is he searching for the diary?* she wondered. Maybe he'd been looking for it all morning in the minutes between classes. She felt kind of bad about that, but it couldn't be helped. He didn't seem mad at her about the pipe, but maybe he had bigger things on his mind at the moment. Like the missing diary! At least he was still here. Principal R hadn't fired or fried him. Not yet, anyway.

But what story would her stepmom have told the principal by now? Had she pinned the blame for the stolen musical pipe on *her*? Or on Wolfgang? Her three BFFs all seemed to believe Wolfgang's innocence in all this. However, Snow wasn't so sure. She was just as suspicious of him as Red seemed to be of *her*!

"Hey," Prince said as he sat down next to her. "Mr. Hump-Dumpty sure seems sunny side down. Must be because of all that stuff that happened in the Great Hall yesterday, huh?"

Snow nodded. "*Eggs*actly." She would've liked to tell him about last night. To fill him in on E.V.I.L., the mapestry, and the discovery of the diary. But the girls had sworn to keep all that secret from everyone for now.

Before she could come up with something she *could* say, Mr. Hump-Dumpty rose from his desk. "Please get out your handbooks and set them for History class," he said. Then he reached out with his walking stick and tapped at the reading assignment written on the board on the wall behind his desk. "You may have the whole period for reading chapter thirteen — Bad Luck Bringers of Olden Times and Nursery Rhymes."

After that announcement, he slumped in his desk chair. Snow and Prince gazed at each other in horror. They both knew that number thirteen was the unluckiest of all numbers. That was *all* she needed today, thought Snow. More bad luck!

Snow reached into her bag. As before, the very thing she wanted — in this case, her handbook — seemed to leap into her hand. With a sigh, she opened her book and dutifully began to read the assigned chapter.

Mr. Hump-Dumpty spent the rest of the period gazing dejectedly around the room without really focusing on anyone or anything. Once in a while he glanced nervously at the classroom door as if expecting someone he'd rather avoid to burst in at any moment. Like Principal R, maybe? Or her stepmom?

Meanwhile, Snow grew more and more tense as she read of cracked mirrors resulting in seven long years of bad luck. Of people who found treasure only to have it stolen. Of partners forever separated because of unlucky wishes they'd made. There were many such stories in Grimmlandia's history.

When the school clock bonged at the end of the period, Snow and Prince both slammed their books shut in relief and leaped up. "Phew! Glad that's over," said Prince. He fell into step with her as they exited the room, flipping his lucky coin in the air and catching it as it fell. He didn't seem to notice that she wasn't wearing her lucky clover amulet. She could *really* use it right about now to make herself feel better. She was about to mention the lost amulet when Prince brought up Saturday's ball.

"Foulsmell told me everyone's calling it the 'Prince Prance,'" he said, sounding more relaxed and amused now. "Did you know?"

Snow nodded, smiling slightly. "Yeah, I heard. Cute nickname, huh?" Out of the corner of her eye, she saw her stepmom walk out of her classroom next door. Ms. Wicked's gaze snagged hers, and like a fly caught in a spider's web, Snow knew there was no escape. Without any lucky charms, her luck had run out! Resigned, she hurriedly smoothed her skirt and straightened the bow on her blouse as her stepmom approached.

Ms. Wicked's hard eyes flicked from Snow to Prince and back again. "Good morning, Prince," she said warmly.

Snow braced herself. But to her surprise, Ms. Wicked actually *beamed* at her and slung an affectionate arm around Snow's shoulders in a quick hug. "I see you've met Snow. She's one of the best and brightest students at the Academy. I'm so lucky to have such a charming, sweet daughter."

Huh? thought Snow, stepping away from the hug as soon as she could. *Daughter*, not *step*daughter? Best and brightest? Why was Ms. Wicked suddenly competing for Stepmother of the Year?

"Anyone would be lucky to have her as a . . . *special friend*," Ms. Wicked went on, giving the prince a wink.

Aghhh! Snow wanted to sink right through the floor! Or run and hide. Or turn back time and put a spell on her step-mom's lips to stop her from saying that. *How grimmiliating!* Why did she have to pick now to gush like this and be so obvious about wanting Prince to be Snow's boyfriend? And why did her stepmom want that anyway?

"Uh, thank you," Prince replied politely.

Snow had always hoped to hear kind motherly — though less embarrassing — words come out of Ms. Wicked's mouth. Still, she didn't trust that her stepmom had really *meant* them. Could she be scheming to get on Prince's good side for some reason? Maybe she was planning to try and recruit him for E.V.I.L. just like she'd (unsuccessfully) tried to do with Prince Awesome not long ago.

It had taken years of life with Ms. Wicked to make Snow so wary. And what she'd overheard last night had multiplied that wariness. She knew that believing her stepmother's honeyed words now would only lead to disappointment in the future. But, oh, how it hurt to admit that!

Sure enough, just as Snow and Prince were turning to go, Snow's stepmom showed her true colors. "So how are those new shoelaces working out for you, sweetie?" she asked with pretended innocence.

"Fine," Snow lied, not willing to give her the satisfaction of knowing the laces had caused her to trip up yesterday. "Only I decided to wear a different pair of shoes today."

"So I noticed," said her stepmom, eyeing Snow's slip-on blue slippers. Then her gaze rose to Snow's hair, and she frowned. "Lucky for you, I have another gift for you," she added. After sliding her large bag from her shoulder, she reached inside it and pulled out a beautiful opal-backed brush. Glancing at Snow's hair again, she said in a super sugary voice, "I figured you must have lost your old brush."

Snow flinched and instantly ran a hand over her hair to smooth it. Did it really look that bad? The opal brush *was* pretty, but as her stepmom held it out to her, Snow hesitated to take it, remembering the laces and other previous gifts that had turned out badly.

"What's wrong?" her stepmom asked in an anxious tone of voice. "Don't you like it?" Ms. Wicked looked at Prince and shrugged, as if to say, *See how Snow snubs me even though I try to be a good mother to her?*

After talking her up before, was her stepmom now trying to make her look bad in his eyes? Snow wondered. *Whatever!* Snow wouldn't let her get away with that. Not *this* time! She sent Ms. Wicked a fake-sweet smile. "It's beautiful. I love it," she said, taking the brush and dropping it into her sparkly blue bag.

Just then, Prince Awesome called Prince Prince away from her side.

"You're welcome," Ms. Wicked told Snow, once he was gone. "Use it in good health." Whirling around in a satisfied swish of black and purple robes, she returned to her classroom.

Use it in good health? What was that supposed to mean?

10

The Crystal Room

Snow frowned down at the contents of the Lost and Found box. As it turned out, she hadn't made it to the office till after school. Classes were over for the day now, and she'd come straight here with fingers crossed.

"No luck?" asked Ms. Jabberwocky, peering into the box from where she sat at her desk.

Snow shook her head. Red's basket had retrieved her agate at lunch, but even having that lucky charm back hadn't brought her enough luck to break the clover necklace free of whatever imprisoned it. Giving up, she pushed the box back onto its shelf. "Nuh-uh. That clover necklace was my luckiest charm, too. I can't believe it's gone." Her disappointment must have shown.

"Cheer up!" Ms. Jabberwocky said, giving Snow one of her big, scary-tooth smiles. "I bet it'll turn up snicker-snack. I'll keep a manxsome eye out for it and let you know if it gets turned in. In the meantime . . ." Ms. Jabberwocky handed Snow a replacement key, so she'd be able to get into her trunker.

"Thanks," said Snow, dropping it into her bag. "I'll be in the library. In case my necklace turns up, I mean." After leaving the office, she climbed up and down stairs all over the Academy searching for the Grimmstone Library.

"Aha!" Her green eyes lit up as she finally spied what she was looking for on the third floor of Gray Castle. A plain brass knob poking from the wall between two classrooms. It was the library doorknob. The only one in the whole school without the Academy logo. It was always tricky to locate since it moved around the school as it pleased.

Snow reached out. The doorknob morphed into the shape of a goose's head as soon as her fingers touched it.

Honk! went the gooseknob. "Ready to riddle?" it asked.

She nodded. Until you answered a riddle, the library door wouldn't appear around the knob.

"Thirty white horses upon a red hill," said the gooseknob. "Now they tramp, now they champ, now they stand still."

"Teeth," said Cinda, who had just come up behind Snow. "The white horses are teeth. It's from a nursery rhyme."

Oh! thought Snow, who hadn't heard the rhyme before. Then that must mean that the red hill represented a tongue. The colors white and red were important clues. "Don't people have thirty-two teeth, though?" she asked.

"Never quibble with a nursery rhyme!" quipped the gooseknob.

Snick! Without another word, it magically turned back into a round brass knob. Immediately, a huge rectangular door drew itself on the wall around the knob. It was several feet taller than Snow and Cinda, about four feet wide, and decorated with carvings of nursery-rhyme characters like Little Bo-Peep with her sheep and Little Boy Blue under a haystack.

As she turned the doorknob, Snow smiled over her shoulder at Cinda. "Good job!" Then the two girls stepped through the doorway. The library could change its size as it pleased, and often did. Right now it was big. Bigger than the Great Hall. Bigger than the entire Academy and the grounds that surrounded it! Yet it magically fit wherever it wanted.

"I see Red and Rapunzel," said Cinda. She and Snow waved to the pair of Grimm girls just beyond the tall desk in the entrance. On the desk were a bell, a gooseneck lamp, and a woven basket full of goose-feather quill pens. Behind the desk stood Ms. Goose, the librarian. She glanced up at the girls as she busily checked in returned books and artifacts, which she pulled one by one from a book drop.

"Good day, goslings!" Ms. Goose greeted them. She was dressed as usual in a frilly white cap and a crisp white apron with a curlicue *L* embroidered on its front bib. *L* for librarian, of course!

Beyond her were rows and rows of shelves and little rooms that stretched far into the distance. They were filled with books and items from *A* to *Z*.

"Do let me know if you need anything," Ms. Goose called after them as they passed her and joined their friends. "Or if you see anything unusual, such as an artifact trying to *V* for vacate the premises with another stolen artifact."

After promising they would, the four girls took off through the *A* section with Red in the lead. There were no windows in the library. Instead, chandeliers hung from its high ceiling, each one lit with dozens of candles. Snow peered at a snow-white goose zooming by high overhead. *Flap! Flap!* Another goose swooped around it and shot off in another direction. Then another swooped in from the right. A net bag dangled from each goose's bright orange beak. Some of the bags held books. Others held objects.

On various shelves in the *A* section, they spotted avocados, apricots, and . . . apples. These weren't items to be checked out, but snacks for hungry library users! Her BFFs each grabbed something to munch. But Snow didn't. Because she was *A* for allergic to fruit, as they all knew. Especially apples!

"Where are we going?" she asked.

"Section *C*," Red replied. "For some *C* for conversation. We're almost there. Don't be mad, but I invited Wolfgang."

"But —" Snow began in dismay.

Red rushed on, interrupting her. "I think you'll want to hear what he told me between rehearsals in Drama class today. And maybe we can clear some things up between us all."

Snow swallowed the rest of her protest. Her friends already knew she distrusted Wolfgang. She could at least wait until she heard what he had to say for himself before issuing any more warnings about him. He certainly had some explaining to do, though, in her opinion.

Bubbles floated around them in the *B* aisles, as the four girls passed boxes and bags, which held bunches of bagpipes and bundles of buns. *Ding dong! Ding dong!* Merry ringing sounds rang out as they passed a room filled with bells. Seconds later, a voice drifted out from another room: "Oh, yeah? Well, *I* can stand on one foot while juggling eight balls, eating a piece of cake, *and* painting a picture." It was a room full of boasts.

As they entered section *C*, Cinda quipped, "I feel so at home here!" Because her name started with *C*, she meant.

"I get it," said Snow. She and the others grinned. Soon they were passing shelves filled with cabbages and calendars, and caps of all colors, shapes, and sizes.

"Here we are," said Red as they reached a sparkly glass door. "The Crystal Room."

Rapunzel paused in the doorway, and then stepped back. "I think I'll go check the *D* section and see if there are any shelves missing a diary."

"Okay, *C* you back here in a few," Cinda joked. She drew an invisible *C* in the air with a fingertip as she spoke, making them all smile again.

As Rapunzel headed off, Red pulled the door open and held it for Snow and Cinda to go first. Snow blinked in wonder at the astonishingly bright room she entered. A circle of large candles, each in a crystal holder, hovered just below its domed glass ceiling, which arched high over their heads. Candlelight bounced off the glass walls and the hundreds of crystal objects that rested on glass tables and shelves, scattering little rainbows all over the room. There were paperweights, miniature crystal unicorns and other fanciful animals, fancy goblets, and dozens and dozens of crystal balls of every shape and color.

Some of the tables and shelves were stationary. Others floated around the room in mid-air. Wolfgang was already in the room waiting for them, sitting at a glass table covered with crystal balls. He'd taken off his wolf-skin jacket and draped it over the back of his chair.

He looked up as the girls joined him, flashing Red a quick grin. Before she could fill him in on their latest news, he piped up with an admission. "I took the Pied Piper's pipe from the library. I gave it to Ms. Wicked hoping she'd finally let me into E.V.I.L. so I can spy on the group."

It was exactly the story Snow had expected from him after what Red had told the girls. But, was it true?

"You didn't plant the pipe on Mr. Hump-Dumpty, though, right?" Red said, glancing around at the other girls.

Studying Snow, Wolfgang shook his head. Had Red told him Snow doubted him?

"Where's the pipe now?" Cinda asked. When Wolfgang shrugged to indicate he didn't know, she plopped down in a chair and started toying with a glass giraffe.

"Probably just escaped on its own," said Red. Ducking a roving shelf of crystal snowflakes, she sat at the table across from Cinda.

Snow sat across from Wolfgang and looked him right in the eye. "Any clue who 'Ell' could be? It's someone my step-mom said she'd be willing to sacrifice you to for the sake of E.V.I.L."

His gray eyes went wide with worry. "No idea. Ell as in Ellen, maybe? Or Eleanor, or . . ."

"Or maybe Ms. Wicked meant the *initial L*," Cinda suggested.

"Oh," said Snow. She hadn't thought of that. But now she snapped her fingers. "*L* could stand for Leader!"

"As in Leader of E.V.I.L.? Ooh! Who could it be?" Red asked. She and Cinda began discussing ideas. Half-listening,

Snow picked a crystal ball at random and twirled it in circles on the table like a top. Then she leaned toward Wolfgang and quietly said, "I guess you know that my step-mom could get you kicked out of the Academy for stealing that pipe."

He shook his head. "Won't happen. She won't tell because she's as guilty as I am! More, actually."

Snow wasn't so sure about that. "No one saw you give Ms. Wicked the pipe, right?"

He nodded. By now, the other two girls had given up on ideas for who the E.V.I.L. leader could be and were just listening to Wolfgang and Snow.

"Then it's your word against hers," Red said, sounding concerned.

"And my stepmom is a very good liar," Snow informed Wolfgang. "She could *definitely* get you kicked out!"

Wolfgang stood and began to walk to and fro, dodging various floating crystal objects as he paced. Finally, he returned and brought up a good point. "Principal R would wonder why she took so long to tell him. When it comes to the Society, he knows more than he lets on. My grandtress, I mean Grandmother Enchantress, told me so."

"Your . . . um . . . *grandtress*?" Snow asked, flashing him a look of confusion.

"That's what I call her for short," Wolfgang explained, half-sitting across from her on one edge of the table.

"Great-great-grandmother takes too long to say. And Grandmother Enchantress is a mouthful, too."

Snow frowned as she gave her crystal ball another spin. Red had never told her that Wolfgang and Grandmother Enchantress were *related*. Cinda didn't seem surprised, though. Did Rapunzel know? Was Snow the only one that hadn't been told? Because Red didn't entirely trust her? Well, that *really* stung.

Avoiding Snow's eyes, Red picked up a crystal dragon and pretended to examine it. *Humph,* thought Snow as she twirled the crystal ball again.

"I hope this missing-pipe disaster doesn't affect my chances of getting into E.V.I.L.," Wolfgang said. "The Society is supposed to vote on my membership tonight."

Just then, Rapunzel burst into the room. "I didn't see any empty spaces where the diary could have been in the *D* section." Her eyes skimmed everyone's faces. "What did I miss?"

"Diary?" echoed Wolfgang.

As Red produced the diary from her basket and showed Wolfgang the inscription, Cinda and Snow filled Rapunzel in on what she missed. "Sorry I couldn't show you the diary during class," Red told Wolfgang. "Someone else might've seen."

"Who do you suppose Lotte G. was?" Rapunzel asked him.

From out of nowhere, a voice replied, "Not was. *Is.*"

Startled, the girls all gasped, wondering where the voice had come from, but Wolfgang only grinned.

Snow's green eyes narrowed on him. Before she could speak, a sparkly pink mist began swirling inside the crystal ball she'd been spinning. She snatched her hands from it in surprise. Suddenly, the ancient, lined face of Grandmother Enchantress appeared in the ball. She looked a little dizzy to Snow. She hoped it wasn't because of all the spinning!

"So *this* is where you've been keeping her crystal ball?" Red asked Wolfgang.

"Not a bad hiding place, huh?" he said, grinning. "Who in E.V.I.L. would think to look for it among all these other crystal balls?"

Snow had to agree he'd chosen well.

"So back to your question, my grandtress wasn't always called Grandmother Enchantress," he told Red with a smile.

"Certainly not," the head in the ball agreed. "I was young once. And back then, my nickname was Lotte. As in Char*lotte*."

"And what did the *G* stand for?" Snow couldn't help asking.

Grandmother Enchantress blinked. "Why, *Grimm*, of course. I'm Wilhelm and Jacob's one and only sister!"

The girls' mouths fell open and Red flashed Wolfgang a look that plainly said, *You should have told me.* Snow couldn't help feeling a bit satisfied. Maybe now Red would understand how it felt when a friend withheld important information!

"I was several years younger than the two of them," the enchantress went on. "But fortunately that didn't stop them from including me in their adventures." A happy, faraway expression came into her eyes.

"So this diary is yours?" Red asked, holding the book up to the ball.

"Indeed," the enchantress confirmed. "I've wondered where it got to all these years. I used to teach Scrying classes in my younger years, and I misplaced it one day."

"Ms. Wicked must have found it," said Snow.

"And she tore a page from it," Cinda informed the enchantress. Red flipped through the pages and showed her where it had been ripped out.

"Oh, dear. I believe that page explained that I'd hidden the mapestry under the tile in the Great Hall," said the grandtress. Her wrinkly face wrinkled even more with worry now as she nodded. "If the Society is searching for the mapestry, that must mean they also plan to search for Grimmlandia's fabled treasure."

"Like us!" said Red.

Rapunzel looked at Wolfgang. "Who all is in the Society anyway? Is Mr. Hump-Dumpty?"

"I don't know," he replied. "That's one of the things I hope to find out by spying on them. All I know now is that Ms. Wicked values his knowledge of Grimmlandia history enough that she gave the diary to him to examine and decide if it was genuine."

Snow nodded. "That makes sense." Her stepmom was shrewd. It was a precaution she would take.

He paused. "When she saw me in the hallway before third period on Wednesday, she asked me to fetch the diary back. Apparently, Mr. Hump-Dumpty wouldn't return it. I asked him for it like she wanted, but had no luck, either."

"I saw you go in there," Snow admitted. "Which later made me suspect you'd been planting the pipe on Mr. Hump-Dumpty."

"Think your stepmom put the pipe in his pocket as payback?" Rapunzel asked.

"Wouldn't put it past her," said Snow, sighing.

"The good news is that the instructions on that diary page won't do anyone in the Society much good since we already found the mapestry under the tile before they could," said Cinda.

"But what will happen when E.V.I.L. discovers that the mapestry isn't there?" Red asked.

"Ah, but perhaps it will be," the grandtress said at last, her eyes twinkling. "If we're in time." Her eyes shifted to

Snow's blue bag, which was sitting on the table right beside the enchantress's crystal ball. It was as if she somehow knew about the tapestry hidden inside!

Red cocked her head. "I don't understand."

Grandmother Enchantress looked over at Snow now and smiled. "Snow will explain."

11

Reflections

Huh? How had Grandmother Enchantress known what she was working on? Snow wondered. But that was the kind of question you simply didn't ask an enchantress. Just like magicians, they had their professional secrets.

"Okay, I have something to show you," Snow announced. Her friends all stared at her as she opened her blue bag. She glanced down into it, and for about a half second she thought she glimpsed some tiny hands waving at her. And grinning bearded faces? Then the fake mapestry practically leaped into her hand. She set it on the table and opened her bag wider, tilting it and causing everything inside to begin tumbling onto the table. On the way out, her handbook fell open. There was a quick flash. *Poof!* Just like that, the figures were gone. *Weird with a beard!*

No one else seemed to have noticed. As they watched her unfold her needlework project, she decided she'd probably only been imagining things because she'd been up so late last night. Tonight she really needed to get more sleep!

When Snow's fake mapestry lay flat on the table at last, Cinda looked puzzled. "A blank piece of tapestry fabric? I don't get it."

"It's a mapestry," Snow explained. "A fake one almost identical to the real one except it's not magic in any way." She ran a finger over it, pointing out and naming the various locations she'd stitched. "You can't see anything yet because I'm using invisible thread to make it."

"Which means that until the mapestry is completely finished, it's only visible to you," said Red.

Snow nodded, then her gaze shifted to the enchantress. "Unless you can see it, too?"

Grandmother Enchantress smiled. "I can, actually. And it's perfect."

Snow glowed under this praise. Just then some of the sparkly pink inside Grandmother Enchantress's crystal ball whooshed out and covered Snow's tapestry project. She pushed back in her chair, surprised. When the pink sparkles evaporated, Red exclaimed, "Hey, I can see your stitching now!"

"Me, too," Rapunzel and Cinda chimed in.

"And me," added Wolfgang.

A feeling of pleasure filled Snow as they crowded around to marvel at it. She started gathering her belongings to stash them back in her bag. Noticing that the opal brush her stepmom had given her had gotten tangled up in some of her thread twist, she began carefully untangling the threads from the brush's bristles.

"Let's compare," said Red, as she opened the hinged lid of her basket and pulled out the real mapestry. Snow continued untangling threads from her brush as she watched Red spread the two stitched maps out side by side on the table.

"Grimmazing!" said Rapunzel.

"The one you're making looks exactly like the *real* one!" Wolfgang told Snow in awe. "You did it from memory?"

Snow nodded. Having successfully untangled the brush and threads, she set them down. Instantly, the brush began tangling itself in the threads again. She gasped. It was another of her stepmom's cruel tricks! If the brush had stayed in her bag much longer its bristles probably would've clawed through the thread twist and the stitches of her tapestry, too. Even through her purse. She hated to think what the brush might have done to her hair if she'd actually used it that morning!

She remembered what her stepmom had said when she'd given it to her. *Use it in good health.* Oh, right! For the second time in less than twenty-four hours, Snow vowed never, ever to trust her stepmom again.

"What's wrong?" Cinda asked her, seeing her expression. The others had all been so focused on the tapestries that they hadn't noticed the brush's behavior.

"Nothing," said Snow. She tossed the brush across the room into a crystal trash can. *Thunk!* Good riddance.

"Score!" Wolfgang cheered.

Snow couldn't help smiling a little at that. "There's still the Great Hall, Pink Castle, and Neverwood Forest left to finish," she said as the others continued to compare the twin mapestries.

"No, your forest is done," Red corrected.

"What?" Looking closely at her mapestry now, Snow did a double-take. It was true, she realized. She didn't recall having stitched the rest of it or getting the wall surrounding it completed, either. But she must have.

"Your stitches are perfect," Cinda said in admiration. "You've even matched the colors."

"I left out your cottage on purpose," Snow told the enchantress. On the real mapestry, a tiny representation of the Enchantress's cottage was smack dab in the middle of the embroidered Neverwood Forest, but Snow's forest just showed trees there. "In case it ever fell into the wrong hands, I didn't want to direct anyone to where you live."

The enchantress nodded in approval. "Good thinking," she said warmly.

"The wrong hands?" Red asked, eyeing Snow with new suspicion. "Why did you make this thing, anyway? How did you know we'd need it?"

Quickly, Snow explained about the crystal ball order form she'd seen Ms. Wicked holding just yesterday morning. "The Society wants a mapestry, so we'll give them one. A fake one," she finished. She was gratified to see some of the suspicion fade from Red's eyes.

"Snow has provided just the right solution to our problem!" Wolfgang's grandtress congratulated her.

"Thanks." Snow smiled. After a slight hesitation, she added, "Only, I'm worried that E.V.I.L. will know my mapestry's a fake when they discover there's no magic in it."

The enchantress smiled back at her from inside the crystal ball. "Not to worry. I'll —"

Suddenly, she looked over her shoulder at something the others couldn't see. "Someone's coming. I must go." She raised one hand and pointed a finger at Snow's fake mapestry. At once, it folded in half and rose from the table. It hovered over the crystal ball for a moment before being sucked inside it.

The girls stared in amazement as the mapestry appeared in the enchantress's hand within the ball. "When the time is right and the mapestry is ready, I'll return it to Wolfgang, so he can put it under the tile in the Great Hall where the Society will surely search for it," she told them. Then she turned away and scurried off, becoming smaller and smaller in the crystal ball. She was only a few inches tall in the crystal ball when she stopped and turned back toward them. "Almost forgot. I'm keeping *this*." As the enchantress spoke, her diary flew from the table and into the crystal ball, where it appeared in her free hand. Then she dashed off again, disappearing into the ball's misty pink cloud.

As Red tucked the real mapestry back into her basket, she said to Wolfgang, "Maybe you should leave the library first. Just in case we run into Ms. Wicked."

Good idea, thought Snow. Her stepmom knew that Wolfgang and Red saw each other for play practice, but she'd be suspicious of him hanging with all four girls.

Wolfgang nodded. "See you, Red Robin," he told Red in a fond, teasing voice. With a wave of farewell to the rest of them, he headed out the glass door of the Crystal Room back into the library. Snow trusted him a bit more now than she had before. But she still didn't trust him completely. Maybe because shape-shifting wolf-boys just didn't seem all that trustworthy!

Minutes later, the four Grimm girls headed out of the Crystal Room, too. Just before they left the library, Snow pulled the others aside. "Something's bothering me about that diary."

Her three friends looked at her expectantly.

"Well, what is it?" asked Rapunzel.

"Are we sure that it's what we were supposed to find?" Snow blurted. "It hasn't been much of a help. Or a treasure clue or anything. Maybe we should still be searching for something else."

"My glass slippers *did* lead us to the diary," Cinda said uncertainly.

"They did," Red agreed. She hesitated. "But maybe Snow's right. I mean, if the diary was what we were supposed to find, it seems like a new trail of golden stitches should have appeared on the real mapestry by now."

"Maybe they're just slow in appearing this time," said Rapunzel.

"Maybe," said Red. "But even though the trail stitches have faded away, the *X* is still there in the same spot as last night. I noticed it just now in the Crystal Room."

"Really?" said Cinda. "I guess I was too busy admiring Snow's duplicate mapestry to see that."

"I didn't notice, either," admitted Snow.

"Nor me," said Rapunzel. Her forehead wrinkled in thought for a moment. "The glass slippers led us to Mr. Hump-Dumpty's *desk*," she said at last.

The girls all looked at one another. Then, without another word, they raced out the library exit, up the halls that were empty by now, and back downstairs to the first floor of Pink Castle and Mr. Hump-Dumpty's room.

Red poked her head in Mr. Hump-Dumpty's door, then looked back at the others. "The coast is clear," she whispered, pushing the door wider. As the girls slipped inside, Snow sneaked next door to peek inside her stepmom's room. Seeing that it was empty, too, she heaved a sigh of relief and rejoined her friends.

"I'll keep a lookout," said Red, waving Snow past her when she came back inside the History classroom. Snow nodded and joined the other two girls as they searched Mr. Hump-Dumpty's desk. There had to be something else in it that was what they were really supposed to find!

"This old desk is so cool," Snow said. "My stepmom told me the ones like this are left over from the time the school was built." Snow ran her hand over one of its drawer fronts, which was carved with an intricate flower and leaf pattern. But she hesitated to open it. It was a teacher's desk, after all.

Rapunzel didn't hesitate one bit. She pulled on an ornate brass handle and opened the center drawer. "Nothing but ink bottles and vellum paper pads," she announced in disappointment.

Snow slowly pulled open a drawer, too. "Same here."

"Ditto," said Cinda, shutting the drawer she'd searched.

Squeak! Snow winced at the sound as she pulled open a bigger bottom drawer. She kneeled and leafed through the papers inside. Mostly old test papers and essays. Then she noticed a bottle of Cracks-be-Gone and some Shell Bandages. "There's some weird stuff in here," she murmured.

Suddenly, Cinda giggled. "I'll say." She had been poking around in the top right drawer and now pulled something out of it. It was a large, floppy, bright yellow bow tie with red, blue, and green polka dots all over it. "Look at this!"

"I don't think I've ever seen Mr. Hump-Dumpty wear that," Red said in a loud whisper from over by the door.

"Good thing, too," quipped Rapunzel. "He'd look like a clown!"

The girls all laughed, and Snow knew they were all picturing Mr. Hump-Dumpty in the bow tie, with huge red lips, baggy trousers, and big shoes.

Cinda hesitated as she started to put the bow tie back inside the drawer. "Think this is what we were supposed to find?"

"I'll check the mapestry," said Red, pushing her basket down her arm so she could open it up. "Nope, the old *X* is still there," she reported back from her post by the door.

Snow had emptied out the bottom drawer by now, but found nothing of real interest. As she was stuffing the folders and papers back inside, however, her hand happened to brush the back of the drawer.

Snap! She let out a gasp as a panel slid up. "There's something behind this drawer. In a secret compartment," she said in excitement. She grasped the silvery object she'd glimpsed and pulled it out to examine it. "A hand mirror!"

Her face fell — and the mirror did, too. When she saw what it was she'd found, she let it drop back into the drawer.

Cinda and Rapunzel gathered around, and Rapunzel picked up the mirror. "It's an old one!" Cinda exclaimed.

"Let me see," said Red. Unable to resist, she'd left her post and come to join them. Rapunzel handed the mirror to her. "It's pretty," Red commented. The silver-backed mirror had an ornate, curlicued edge around it, which was repeated on its handle. The back was etched with silver roses.

"Doesn't look like something Mr. Hump-Dumpty would use, though," Snow put in.

"Maybe it's not his," said Red. "Maybe he doesn't even know it's in here." She held it out to Snow.

But Snow shook her head. "I'm not touching it again," she said, backing away from the others. "You know mirrors weird me out."

Cinda took it instead. "Do you suppose it's magic?" she asked. As Cinda flipped the hand mirror around, Snow saw her reflection in it briefly and quickly looked away.

"Of course I'm magic," said a sharp, smooth voice, drawing everyone's attention.

Oh, no, thought Snow as a ghostly, shiny, silvery face appeared on the surface of the mirror. *Not* another *talking mirror!*

The face in the mirror peered at the girls. "Ooh-ee! It's nice to be out of that drawer. I've been cooped up in there for an eternity. And I'm much too gorgeous to be hidden away. I mean, have you seen my silver backside?"

"Huh?" said Snow. This mirror belonged back in the library's *B* for boastful section!

"So, what does your magic do, if you don't mind my asking?" said Cinda.

The ghostly image's eyebrows rose. "I can show you reflections of the truth anytime you're uncertain what to believe," it said.

Rapunzel frowned at the mirror. "Reflections of the truth?" she repeated. "Just what exactly is that supposed to mean?"

But before the mirror could reply, the girls heard a door slam somewhere out in the hallway. "We'd better get out of here before we're discovered," Rapunzel warned the others in a low voice. "So, do we take the mirror or what?"

"Don't put me back in that drawer," the mirror begged. "I belong to the one who found me. If she doesn't take me with her, I'll crack up."

Everyone, including the mirror, looked at Snow.

"You know I hate mirrors," Snow said quickly, but then she immediately wished she could take back the words. She hoped she hadn't hurt the hand mirror's feelings. If it had any.

"Yeah, we know," said Rapunzel. "I've always wondered why."

"Because my stepmom loves them," Snow admitted.

"They are useful," said Cinda. "For trying out gowns and makeup."

"But how many mirrors do you need? My stepmom has about a hundred," Snow continued. "And I feel like they're always watching me."

The other girls stared at her.

"A hundred?" Red echoed.

"Watching you?" said Rapunzel.

Snow nodded, a little embarrassed at their stares. "There were mirrors in every room of the castle when I was little. And you know the full-length one that's turned sideways in the Scrying classroom? The one my stepmom writes assignments on in red lipstick instead of using a whiteboard like normal teachers? Well, it used to be in the castle where we lived. And she *talked* to it. A lot. It was like her best bud or something. It kind of gave me the willies."

"Well, boo-hoo. Get over it," the mirror admonished her lightly. "Like I said, because you found me, I belong to you. Mirror rules."

"Are you her magic charm?" asked Cinda.

Rapunzel elbowed her gently. "Magic charms can't talk, remember?"

"Nope, not a charm. Lucky for you, though, that I *can* talk," the mirror told Snow. "Because I've got secrets I can tell. Secrets you'll want to know," it coaxed in a sing-song voice.

While it was gabbing away, Red had opened her basket and taken out the mapestry. Now she held it out to the others. "The *X* is gone!" she exclaimed. "But I don't see a new trail of stitches yet."

"Still, it must mean that this mirror is what we were meant to find," said Rapunzel.

Right then, they heard another noise somewhere down the hall. Closer this time.

"Someone's coming!" hissed Cinda.

"Quick! Hide the mirror and let's scram," said Red.

The mirror jumped into Snow's blue bag before anyone could act. In a panic to go before they were all caught, she grabbed the bag and headed for the door. As the girls scurried down the hall, she heard the mirror's muffled voice from inside her bag.

"Oh, hi. I like handbooks and pens, and lip gloss is okay. But I don't really get along with scarves. And there are seven of you? Oh, well. I guess a mirror must make do."

Scarves? thought Snow. She didn't have any scarves in her bag. No, she must've misheard. Although she couldn't think of another word that even came close.

12

The Silver Blob

"Stop!" Rapunzel half-ordered, half-pleaded when the four friends reached the grand staircase. "I can't go up to the tower right now. I'm sorry, okay? Let's go somewhere else."

Honestly! thought Snow. Rapunzel's fear of heights was a real problem sometimes. Like now, when they were in a hurry. "Okay," she said. "So where can we go instead? We need someplace close."

Before they could decide anything, they heard the noise they'd heard before. *Step. Thump. Step.*

"That sounds like Mr. Hump-Dumpty coming!" exclaimed Cinda. "Yikes!"

The Grimm girls did an about-face back down the first floor hall.

"In here," said Rapunzel. She opened the nearest door and they all dashed in. It turned out to be a supply closet right across the hall from Ms. Wicked's classroom. Inside, there were unused teacher and student desks, a flowered couch with a hole in its fabric, a couple of tables, as well as lamps and bookcases. The wooden arms of the couch were singed black. *Perhaps it had once sat in Ms. Jabberwocky's office,* thought Snow.

Suddenly, everything turned pitch-black inside the closet as Rapunzel shut the door to the hall. All four girls put their ears to the door. *Step. Thump. Step.* They heard whistling, then the sound of a broom being pushed. Soon, the sounds began fading away.

"It was only Mr. Winkie," said Rapunzel, sounding relieved. "I think he went upstairs. So why don't we just talk in here? Seems safe enough."

Snick! After fumbling around, Cinda managed to locate and turn on one of the oil lamps stored in the room. Right away, Red pulled the mapestry out of her basket. "Let's see if there's a new trail of golden stitches yet," she explained as the others watched her unroll it.

"Yes!" the girls cried in unison. For a new golden thread-path now snaked from Pink Castle to the grounds outside it. The new path followed along the Once Upon River before ending in a new *X* cross-stitch atop a heart-shaped island downstream from Maze Island.

Cinda tapped at the *X* with a finger. "That's Heart Island, right? I haven't been to it yet. Maybe we'll find the treasure there. Since we didn't find it in Mr. Hump-Dumpty's room."

All at once, Snow glimpsed something tiny and grayish

moving across the surface of the mapestry. She whisked her hand across it, thinking that a bug had landed on the mapestry. But a second glance told her that this was no bug. A tiny embroidered silver blob was gliding across the stitched representation of Pink Castle. "Look!" she said, pointing to the blob.

"Is that the hand mirror?" Red asked, confused. The mapestry *had* traced the movements of Peter Peter's pumpkin (showing it as a tiny embroidered orange blob) when it changed into a stagecoach and disappeared into Neverwood Forest.

"Quick," Rapunzel said to Snow. "See if you still have it!"

As soon as Snow opened her bag, the mirror sailed out of it. Almost like it had been *thrown* out of the bag, instead of leaping out on its own. "Whoa! Careful! I can break, you know! Do you really *want* seven years of bad luck?" it shouted at the bag.

That mirror is getting odder by the minute, Snow thought. She caught it by its handle before it could fall. Not wanting to look at her own reflection, she held it so it faced the mapestry and her friends, not her. But when her friends' eyes fell on the mirror's shiny surface, they gasped.

"What?" asked Snow. When she moved her head to see what they saw in the mirror, she gasped, too. Because its reflection of the mapestry clearly showed that the silver blob was actually a tiny embroidered silver *pail*. All at once, what the mirror had said came back to her: *I can show you reflections of the truth anytime you're uncertain what to believe.*

"That silver blob is Jack and Jill's missing pail!" Snow exclaimed. They all watched the mirror in fascinated horror as the pail-shaped silver blob glided over the castle drawbridge, then disappeared around the side of Pink Castle.

Moments later, the blob reappeared on the mapestry, moving between the green-stitched trees of Neverwood Forest. And then, just like what had happened with Peter Peter's pumpkin, the embroidered pail hit the stitched wall that surrounded Grimmlandia and vanished off the edge of the mapestry altogether!

The Grimm girls had feared before now that the pail might have already met the same fate as Peter Peter's pumpkin, but still they stared at the mapestry in stunned disbelief. "Well, that's that, then," Rapunzel said glumly. "The pail's gone."

"Sorry," the mirror told them. "I can only reflect truth."

Dismayed, Snow bit her lip. "We understand." *How much weaker would the protective spells keeping Grimmlandia safe become, now that one more magical object has gone over the wall?* she wondered. Was the end of Grimmlandia in sight? Would they all be swallowed up in the Nothingterror? How many more artifacts would have to disappear to completely sever the boundaries between the two worlds? Three? Two? Only one? She shivered as she slid the now-silent hand mirror back inside her bag.

At the same time, Red rolled up the mapestry and stuck it back in her basket. Her shoulders slumped. "If only we could have stopped it from happening!" Hearing that, her basket slung itself onto her arm and nestled close to Red's side as if trying to comfort her.

Suddenly, they heard more footsteps, lighter than Mr. Winkie's, out in the hall. Someone knocked. The girls clung to one another and stared at the closet door with wide eyes, sure they were about to be discovered. Who was out there? How would they explain their presence here? They couldn't! But then they heard another door somewhere out in the hall open up instead. It had only *sounded* like the knocking was on the supply closet door.

Still huddled together, they heard Malorette's shrill voice cry out, "We did it, Ms. Wicked!"

Huh? Snow gave a start. In the dim closet, the four girls gazed at each other with wide, surprised eyes.

"Jack and Jill's pail has gone over the wall!" Odette's voice crowed.

Cinda's lip curled. "My stepsisters," she hissed through clenched teeth. "Figures they'd have a hand in this catastrophe."

Red put a finger to her lips to shush her.

140

"They must be standing outside Ms. Wicked's class-room," Rapunzel whispered.

It had been empty earlier. *My stepmom must have sneaked in while we were busy in Mr. Hump-Dumpty's room,* thought Snow. Good thing she hadn't caught them!

And now Ms. Wicked spoke up, sounding excited. "Excellent news! Our leader will be well pleased with us. But such things should not be discussed here in the open. I'll inform him myself since we meet to discuss another matter tonight."

"Grimmtastic!" said Malorette's voice.

"Nuh-uh. That's about as far from grimmtastic as you can get!" Snow murmured. Her BFFs nodded.

Then the door shut and the sound of the two girls' foot-steps and their soft, excited conversation faded down the hall. After a few more minutes of quiet, Rapunzel slowly opened the closet door and peeked out. "All clear," she murmured. "Let's head to dinner. I've had enough drama for tonight."

"I have, too, for once," said Red.

The girls slipped out. Still a little spooked by all that had happened, they ran down the hall in the direction of the Great Hall.

Snow was the last one out of the closet. As she passed the door to her stepmom's classroom, she stopped dead, staring. The brass door knob with the GA logo on it was changing. Was the library in the process of moving there? It was a shift she'd never seen in action before. However, the logo did not disappear. Instead, the knob went misty and foggy. Then it turned almost transparent.

A long nose poked out from it, startling Snow. It wasn't a goose beak like the library knob usually had, but a person's nose. As if the nose wasn't creepy enough, it quickly withdrew and a brown eye peered out at her through the mist in its place. She stumbled back, pressing a hand to her mouth to stifle a scream.

She didn't wait around for a mouth to appear on the knob. Who knew what it might say to her! Heart pounding, she raced after her friends, hardly daring to breathe until she caught up with them in the Great Hall. After grabbing a tray and some silverware with shaking hands, she joined the line right behind the other three girls.

"Guess what I just saw!" she whispered to Cinda, who was closest. Hearing the excitement and fear in her voice, Red and Rapunzel dropped back. The four of them bunched together as they slowly moved along the line toward the food up ahead.

As Snow quickly described what she'd seen, Cinda paled. "That sounds like the same nose and eyeball I saw in the Grimm brothers room of the library on my first day at the Academy."

"But how could it have moved from there to my step-mom's classroom door?" asked Snow. "And who do the nose and eyeball belong to?"

Red's forehead wrinkled in thought as they all pushed their trays along. After glancing around to make sure no one was listening in, she said in a low voice, "Maybe to *L*. I mean, to E.V.I.L.'s *Leader*, that is."

Rapunzel shuddered, causing her long hair to sway back and forth. "Paying a visit to Ms. Wicked, perhaps? To talk about the pail poaching? And Wolfgang's interest in joining the Society?"

"Makes sense," Cinda agreed.

"Know what I think?" Snow said as a horrible new thought entered her mind. "Grandmother Enchantress once told us that someone *outside* the wall was probably helping E.V.I.L., right? Maybe that someone is the Leader of the Society, who is actually *outside* of Grimmlandia looking in through weak spots in the school that have already lost their protection due to artifacts escaping!"

13

Happy Birthday?

The next morning, Snow left her blue bag in her trunker, taking only her handbook before going off to her Friday classes. The magic hand mirror would be safe there, locked inside her trunker. And far away from her. She was pretty annoyed at that mirror. It had kept her awake last night, making muffled sounds inside her bag as if it were arguing with itself about something. *Weird!*

Six classes and one Great Hall dinner later, she was back at her trunker again. Grabbing her blue bag, she stashed her handbook in it, in case she actually had time to do homework later on. She thought about taking the hand mirror out of her bag and leaving it inside her trunker. But although she still didn't like mirrors, the magic mirror might come in handy when she caught up with Cinda, Red, and Rapunzel in the Grimmstone Library. They were all four meeting there to choose ball gowns for the Prince Prance. And since the mirror could show you reflections of the truth when you weren't sure what to believe, maybe it could help her decide if her friends were just being kind when they told her a gown looked grimmazing on her, or if the gown really *did* look grimmazing. Her stepmom's criticisms lately had made her unsure about her fashion choices.

But when Snow reached inside her blue bag for the mirror she also found something inside it that she wasn't expecting. The mapestry! The real one or the fake one? She looked up and down the hall to be sure no one was watching, then opened her bag wider to check. It was the fake. She could tell because its canvas backing was a lighter color than the backing on the real mapestry. Besides, she knew Red still had the real one. But why had Grandmother Enchantress magicked this thing to *her*, instead of to Wolfgang? Wasn't he supposed to give it to E.V.I.L.?

As she unrolled the mapestry further, a crystal marble the size of a cherry fell out of it and rolled onto the floor. Snow picked it up and held it in her palm. It was a message-marble! Slowly, it grew into a ball of gray mist as big as her hand. Black letters formed in the mist, unfurling across it in a long line. Quickly, she read them before they could disappear for good:

> *Dear Snow,*
>   *Change of plans. The Society is suspicious of Wolfgang and watching him. They checked under the*

floor tile in the Hall. What they wanted was missing of course. Improvise as best you can to get this into your stepmom's hands. Good luck! Signed, Lotte G (Grandmother Enchantress)

Poof! When Snow finished reading, the mist disappeared and only the crystal marble remained. *What am I supposed to do now?* she wondered in dismay. She was no good at improvising. Red was the drama queen, not her! She tossed the marble into her trunker and finished unrolling the fake mapestry. She saw at once that it had been completed. Neverwood Forest, the wall around it, Once Upon River, Pink Castle, the Great Hall, and other parts of Grimmlandia. It was all there.

Suddenly, golden stitches magically appeared, crisscrossing it! Was Grandmother Enchantress controlling them from afar? The stitched paths didn't lead to any of the places the real mapestry had taken them to. They were probably bogus — meant to fool E.V.I.L.!

"Um — can I see you for a sec?" a boy's voice asked her.

Startled, Snow jumped about a mile high. Ramming the mapestry into her bag, she looked up to see that Prince Prince was standing beside her. All of her attention had been on the fake mapestry, so she hadn't noticed him coming over.

"Threads class project gone awry?" he guessed, nodding toward her bag where she'd stashed the mapestry.

She was acting really guilty, she realized. She forced herself to relax and even managed a small laugh. "Exactly," she told him. She swung the bag's strap over her shoulder, shut her trunker, and locked its door with her key and the accompanying rhyme. "No one should see that mapest — I mean — *tap*estry project of mine. It's a tragically hideous mess I'll have to undo."

His lips parted like he was going to speak. But before he could comment, she rushed on. "So what's up? I was just about to meet my friends in the library. We're getting new gowns especially for your ball. And we don't have much time since it's tomorrow, so . . ." She started sidling away. It wasn't that she didn't want to hang with Prince, it was just that she really needed to go show the mapestry to her Grimm girl friends and get some advice. Maybe one of them would have a good idea of how to follow the enchantress's wishes.

"Wait. Before you go, there's something I need to show you first over in Gray Castle," Prince told her. "Please? You won't be sorry."

Seeing how earnest he was, Snow gave in and followed him down the hall toward the far side of the Academy. He walked quickly to get wherever they were going, yet still managed to skillfully flip and catch his lucky coin over and over. He'd been sympathetic about the loss of her clover amulet when he'd finally noticed she wasn't wearing it during Balls class earlier in the day. Was it possible he'd found it and wanted to surprise her with it?

Snow allowed herself to feel a spark of hope about that. "So where exactly are we going?" she asked as they neared the Gray Castle grand staircase.

"You'll see," he said with a mysterious grin. He pulled a piece of vellum paper from his pocket, consulted it, and then started up the stairs. "C'mon."

It had looked to her like there was a simple hand-drawn map on the paper. Strange. She had no idea what was going on or where they were going. When they reached the fourth-floor landing, Prince pushed through the door and started down the hall. Snow hesitated to follow him. This was where all the teachers at the Academy had their living quarters. She caught up with him just as he stopped — right in front of the door to her stepmom's rooms!

"We're here!" he announced with a broad smile. Then to her astonishment and horror, he knocked on the door.

She started backing away. "Wait. What's this all a —"

But before she could finish, her stepmom threw open the door. "Happy Birthday!" Ms. Wicked and Prince called out to Snow at the same time.

She stared back and forth between them in confusion. "But it's not my bir —"

"Thanks for bringing her," interrupted Ms. Wicked. She

beamed at Prince. Then before Snow could say another word, her stepmom reached out, grabbed her hand, and pulled her inside. Then she shut the door in Prince's surprised face.

Snow clutched her bag to her chest and stared at Ms. Wicked in disbelief. "You told him it was my birthday? It's not. Why would you do that?" Her birthday wasn't for several more months.

Her stepmom shrugged. "I wanted to see you."

Snow frowned. "You couldn't have just *asked* me to come by?"

"Would you have?" Her stepmom arched an eyebrow, pouting. "You always make excuses not to visit. Sometimes I think you go out of your way to avoid me."

Snow said nothing. It was an accusation she couldn't exactly deny. She *did* try to avoid her stepmom whenever she could. And besides, this apartment was creepy. The walls were hung with mirrors of all sizes and shapes, big and small, round and narrow. Nary a single inch of wall was without one. It made Snow's skin crawl.

Ms. Wicked pointed toward a black-and-white striped couch. "Have a seat. I think it's time for a little heart-to-heart chat."

Despite Snow's misgivings — for one thing, she wasn't convinced her stepmom *had* a heart — she sat down on the couch next to her stepmom's big, strange, stylish purse.

Luckily, Magic, her stepmom's enormous black cat, was nowhere in sight at the moment. Snow liked Rapunzel's cats, but she and Magic had never gotten along. That bratty cat had scratched and even bitten her dozens of times. It wouldn't have surprised her to learn that Magic was also a member of E.V.I.L.!

"Lemonade?" her stepmom offered, holding up a glass pitcher. There was a plate of delicious-looking cupcakes with glossy white frosting and rainbow sprinkles on the table beside it.

Hic! Hic! Just the smell of the tart lemonade was enough to start Snow hiccupping.

Ms. Wicked gave her head a shake. "Oops! Sorry. I almost forgot you're allergic. No fruit." She set the pitcher down on the ebony coffee table in front of the couch but continued to stand, looming over Snow.

Snow fidgeted. "S'okay. I'm not thirsty, anyway," she said, wondering what her stepmom *really* wanted. She didn't buy the "heart-to-heart chat" for one second. "I can't stay long. My friends are waiting for me in the library to pick out our gowns for tomorrow's ball."

"Oh, how nice. You should avoid getting something with lots of sparkles, though," Ms. Wicked advised.

"Why? I like sparkles," Snow said.

"Yes, I know, dear," her stepmother said with a smarmy sort of smile that bordered on a smirk. "But they're just so . . . *vulgar*. When you wear them, it's like you're shouting out, 'Look at me!'" Her critical eye scanned Snow up and down. "And it might be best not to draw too much attention to your unfortunate figure, sweetie. Don't you agree?"

In the past, such remarks would have made Snow crumple. They would have reduced her to a quivering mass of jelly. But now she sat bolt upright. She didn't need to take this. She'd had it with her stepmom's criticisms. A new spark of confidence welled up inside her and came tumbling out in her words.

"No, I don't agree," she replied firmly. "I feel pretty when I wear sparkles. And that's all that matters." It had felt so good to assert herself this way, that she went on. "In fact, I'm happy with all my choices," she blurted out. "I like my clothes, my friends, and my whole *life!*"

A startled expression flitted across Ms. Wicked's beautiful face. Then she seemed to recover. She smiled sweetly. "Maybe you think that I'm harder on you than on anyone else. Is that what's got your feathers so ruffled? Well, it's only because I care about you so much." She hesitated, peering down at Snow through long black lashes, as if waiting to see what effect her speech was having.

Though Snow had vowed never, ever to trust her stepmom again, these words still tugged at her heart. Especially since they echoed what she'd been telling herself for years to make herself feel better. But if her stepmom expected her to fall into line again, and meekly accept every criticism she dished out, well, it just wasn't going to happen. So Snow simply folded her arms, saying nothing.

Luckily, Ms. Wicked didn't seem to notice her silence. She came closer. Facing the couch where Snow sat, she studied herself in the large, antique, gold-framed mirror that hung on the wall behind it.

Snow watched her stepmom's face as Ms. Wicked patted her tall hairdo approvingly. Then she leaned down to her handbag on the couch and drew a bright red tube from it. As she began to freshen her lipstick, she spoke, changing the subject. "There are forces at this school that you know nothing about," she told Snow lightly.

"You mean the E.V.I.L. Society?" Snow blurted. Then she clapped a hand over her mouth. *Oops!* But it had felt kind of good to finally say it. To get it out in the open, once and for all.

Surprise flashed across her stepmom's face, but then quickly disappeared. Feigning innocence, she said, "I'm not sure what you mean. I believe such a society *did* exist around the time the Grimm brothers established the Academy, but it died out long ago." She pulled a piece of tissue from a box on the coffee table, and then blotted her lips.

So much for openness, thought Snow. "Well . . ." She reached for her blue bag, intending to say good-bye and go. Her friends were waiting for her, after all. But as she reached for her bag, it fell over on its side. And the fake mapestry just popped out on its own and rolled open on the couch. It was almost as if it had been *pushed* out!

Instantly, Ms. Wicked pounced on it, snatching it up in her long fingers. "Where did you get this?" she demanded as her eyes roved greedily over the stitchery.

Improvise as best you can to get this into your stepmom's hands, Grandmother Enchantress's marble-message had said. Having no choice now, Snow concentrated on *improvising* an answer to Ms. Wicked's question.

"My friends and I found it," she said. Which was true, of course. "It's a map, isn't it? Do you think it could be valuable?" she asked, pretending to be clueless.

"It's a mapestry," Ms. Wicked said, surprising Snow with the truth. "It will lead to a treasure beyond your wildest dreams."

Snow couldn't believe it. Not only had her stepmom fallen for the fake mapestry, she'd decided to tell her about it! *But why?* she wondered.

"Grimmlandia is a small world," said Ms. Wicked. Her voice had turned dreamy, almost as if she were talking to herself and had momentarily forgotten Snow. "But it could be larger. Much, much larger." Her eyes brightened at the prospect.

"You mean if Grimmlandia expanded beyond the wall? But that wouldn't necessarily be a good thing, would it?"

Snow ventured. "What about the Dark Nothingterror?" Why was her stepmom telling her all this?

"Oh, *that*," her stepmom said, flicking her fingers dismissively. "Forget all you've ever heard about it. The stories are pure fairy-tale nonsense. Believe me, there'd be nothing to fear if Grimmlandia merged with the Dark Nothingterror. In fact, it would broaden everyone's horizons!"

"Your horizons are broadening a little too much, don't you think?" a small voice snapped at Ms. Wicked. "Maybe you should lay off the cupcakes."

Both Snow and her stepmom's eyes flew to the couch again, where, for some strange reason, the silver hand mirror was now poking out of Snow's bag.

"How dare you!" Ms. Wicked tossed the mapestry to the coffee table, then plucked the mirror from Snow's bag. Holding it by its handle, she glared into it. "Normally, I adore talking mirrors, but where did you get this awful thing, Snow?"

"I, um, bought it at Old Mother Hubbard's Cupboard," Snow *improvised*. The Cupboard was a small market tucked in a corner of Pink Castle. "I'm, uh, trying to get over my fear of mirrors."

"Well, it's about time," Ms. Wicked said with approval.

"Hey! I belong to Snow," the mischievous mirror argued. "I'm not a plaything to be passed around willy-nilly!"

"You'll do as I like, or you'll be sorry," Ms. Wicked

threatened. She made as if to throw it against the wall. Snow half-rose to stop her. Luckily, for once, the mirror clammed up. Appearing pleased by its obedience, Ms. Wicked relaxed and studied herself in the hand mirror as she stood before her larger mirror on the wall. Relieved, Snow sank back down to the couch. Even if the mirror was a bit annoying, she still didn't want to see it destroyed!

"Believe it or not, I'm hoping that you and I can be a team from now on," Ms. Wicked continued to Snow. She fluffed her hair with one hand to make it stand up even higher above the sharp points of her tiara.

A *team*? Snow's brow furrowed. Wasn't that something she had longed for, too? For a few seconds she wondered if her stepmom could be right about there being nothing to fear from a merger between Grimmlandia and the Dark Nothingterror. Could the history in her Grimm Academy Handbook and Grandmother Enchantress be wrong after all? No. She just didn't think so.

"I meant what I said yesterday about you being one of the best and brightest students at the Academy," her step-mother said, still primping in front of the hand mirror. She smiled at Snow and her smile certainly *looked* genuine. Only, Snow wasn't quite buying it. Not this time.

Ms. Wicked twirled around so that her back was to Snow. That way she could check the back of her hairdo by glancing in the hand mirror at her reflection in the big wall mirror. "Think of it," she cajoled. "Just the two of us. Working together to find the treasure."

At that moment, Snow caught sight of her stepmother's reflection in the hand mirror. And she gasped. Because the look in Ms. Wicked's eyes wasn't kind and sweet at all. Instead it was hard and calculating, and the smile curving her lips was unmistakably cruel.

I can show you reflections of the truth whenever you're uncertain what to believe, the magic mirror had said.

"We could work together to find you the perfect gown if you like, too. I want you to have a terrific time at the ball," her stepmom went on. And though she sounded delighted at the idea, her reflection in the hand mirror — narrowed eyes and a sneering smile — revealed her *true* feelings. "Oh, I must say, I really can't improve my appearance any further. Let's just consult your little mirror on the matter and hope it has learned some manners by now. Shall we?" With that, she asked the mirror:

"Mirror, Mirror in my hand.
Who's the fairest in the land?"

How many times had Snow heard her stepmom say these very words? And her mirrors always answered the same way, telling her stepmom that she was beautiful. Because she was, of course! Beautiful, but cruel.

The hand mirror began to speak its reply. But this time, the words it spoke were different from what all the other mirrors had replied:

"You were the fairest long ago.
But now it is the girl named Snow."

Snow leaped to her feet. "What?"

At the same time her stepmom let out a little shriek. "Take your horrible, lying mirror away!" She threw it to the couch. It bounced, but Snow caught it before it could hit the floor and break. She tucked it into her blue bag.

An awkward silence fell. Snow didn't have to see her stepmom's reflection this time to guess how she really felt. *Humpf!* Her stepmom was jealous! Of *her*. She couldn't just be happy for Snow even once!

"I really have to go," Snow said in as calm a voice as she could muster. "My friends will be waiting for me." She rose to her feet.

"Oh, certainly," said Ms. Wicked, smoothing the hair at the back of her neck. She managed a smile. "I'm glad we had this little chat. And I'll just keep the mapestry, shall I?" She nodded toward where it lay open on the coffee table. "I'm so looking forward to searching for the treasure with your help."

Her help? *No way!* thought Snow. She wondered why

Ms. Wicked didn't ask Malorette or Odette to help instead. But then, in a flash, the most likely answer came to her. If they and the other members of E.V.I.L. didn't know about the mapestry, her stepmother wouldn't have to share the treasure with them if she *did* find it. She was so evil she'd even double-cross the E.V.I.L. Society!

"You can keep the mapestry," Snow said. "But . . ." *Hey!* Why was her stepmom so ready to trust her to help with the treasure hunt, anyway? she suddenly wondered. But she had no answer.

"By the way, you and your friend Red might want to keep away from that boy Wolfgang," Ms. Wicked went on.

Distracted by this, Snow set the matter of the treasure aside, "Oh? Why?"

Her stepmom frowned. "Let's just say he comes from a bad family."

Bad family? What about Snow's *own* family? Had her stepmom looked in a mirror lately? Oh, wait, silly question. She never *stopped* looking in mirrors! Ms. Wicked probably thought what she'd said was true though. In her twisted view, Grandmother Enchantress was probably "bad." Had she investigated Wolfgang's family background and learned that the enchantress was his great-great-grandmother? That might explain why she'd become suspicious of him!

"No family is perfect," Snow said carefully. "Well . . ." She took a step toward the door.

"Wait! I almost forgot," Ms. Wicked said, snapping her fingers. She lifted the plate of rainbow-sprinkled cupcakes and held it out to Snow. "Though it's not really your birthday, I made these especially for you. Please do take one."

"I'm not really hungry." Seeing that her stepmom appeared ready to insist, Snow grabbed one anyway. "Okay, I'll eat it on the way to the library. I really do need to go gown shopping now, though." True to form, Ms. Wicked didn't even bother to ask what kind of gown Snow planned to wear to the ball. Nor did she ask how she was doing in her classes, or anything about her friends. It was just *sooo* typical of her!

Ms. Wicked stepped between Snow and the door. "Don't you want to try even one tiny bite before you go? It'll hurt my feelings if you don't," she said in a voice that Snow was sure had more sugar in it than the cupcake.

"Whatever," said Snow. Her stepmother was pretty good at baking actually. She sniffed at the cupcake. *Mmm. Cinnamony.* She licked its frosting, which was grimmilicious. Finally, she opened her mouth and took a big bite.

Ms. Wicked smiled. "There. That should do it." As she opened the door to let Snow into the hall, she added, "One day I'm hoping that you'll come round to seeing things *my* way, dear girl. Because things may get pretty uncomfortable for you until you do."

"Yeah," said Snow. Of course, her reply made no sense, but she just wanted to get out of there and back to her friends!

However, as she climbed downstairs to the Great Hall she regretted that cupcake soon enough. *Hic! Hic!* Her skin began to feel itchy and hot. *Hic! Hic!* Grabbing the mirror from her bag, she held.it in front of her.

Snow stared at her reflection in dismay. *Hic! Hic!* A blotchy red rash had broken out all over her face and neck and down her arms.

The mirror's ghostly face appeared and gazed back at her, aghast. "Yikes!" it said. "No offense, but you'd scare a scarecrow."

It was true. No way could she go to the ball tomorrow looking like this. *Hic! Hic! Hic!*

"Drat my stepmom! There must've been pieces of *apple* in that stupid cupcake!" she moaned. Suddenly, she remembered the prediction her Scrying class mirror had made only two days ago:

"This may come as a giant blow.
But to the ball you will not go."

Hic! Hic! Hic! Tears filled her eyes. That prediction was coming true!

14

Gifts

On Saturday night, Snow was lying in bed at the Academy's infirmary when her three friends came into her room. They hadn't been allowed to visit her until now because those who were jointly in charge of the infirmary — the doctor, the nurse, and the alligator-purse lady — first had to weigh in on a diagnosis and treatment plan.

It had gone like this:

"Mumps," said the doctor.

"Measles," said the nurse.

"Hiccups," said the lady with the alligator purse.

The alligator-purse lady had guessed closest. Because Snow obviously did have the hiccups. But her rash had nothing to do with mumps or measles. When she'd finally gotten things under control enough to be able to speak without hiccupping between every other word, she'd explained to them about her fruit allergy. However, as a precaution in case she really did have something contagious, they'd pronounced that she wasn't allowed to go to the ball tonight. And that was that.

As soon as her friends entered the infirmary, they raced to her bedside and hugged her. "I'm so sorry this happened!" Cinda exclaimed.

"We would have been here sooner," Rapunzel added, "but they made us wait twenty-four hours in case you were contagious."

"Does it hurt?" Red asked, eyeing the rash.

Snow managed a smile. "Not really. It doesn't even itch that much anymore." The infirmary lady had produced a special ointment from her alligator purse that had instantly soothed the rash.

When Snow had gotten up the courage to look at herself in the talking hand mirror just before her friends arrived, she'd seen that the blotches on her skin were more pink than red now. The doctor said it would take a few days for it to completely disappear, but they were already fading. "You won't win any beauty contests tonight," the mirror had told her. "But you're still the fairest in my opinion." Which had been really sweet of that mirror.

"You all look grimmsolutely grimmtastic!" Snow told the three Grimm girls. They were dressed for the ball in ruffled silk and satin gowns. Gowns that glittered with sparkles, Snow noted with satisfaction. Which proved Ms. Wicked *wasn't* the best or only authority on fashion!

"We wish you could come with us," Rapunzel said. Her gown was black, as usual, but for once she'd added a bit of color to her outfit. The blue sash at her waist matched the blue streaks in her hair. And her stylish ankle boots had sparkly blue clasps up their sides.

"We feel awful that you have to miss the ball," Cinda put in. She was pretty in pink tonight in a gown featuring gauzy sleeves and shiny satin ribbons at her waist and neck. Her glass slippers peeked out under the scalloped hem of her gown.

"It just doesn't seem fair," Red added. Her red-and-white striped gown rustled as she sat on the edge of the bed.

A sudden lump rose in Snow's throat. She ran a hand over her soft blue nightgown. It was cute, with white polka dots. But not anywhere near as cute as a ball gown! She felt tears form in her eyes and forced them back. It *wasn't* fair that she couldn't go to the Prince Prance. But no way did she want what had happened to her to cast a shadow on her friends' fun tonight. And she would not to give in to self-pity.

"Horrible things happen," she said with a smile. "But there will be other balls."

"I just don't get how this happened," Red said. She reached over to straighten the flowers in the vase on Snow's bedside table.

"Yeah, you're always so careful to stay away from fruit," said Cinda, as she fluffed Snow's pillow.

"It has something to do with your stepmom, right?" asked Rapunzel as she smoothed Snow's blanket. "We ran into Prince last night in the library. He told us how Ms. Wicked had asked him to bring you upstairs for a birthday surprise, so you were going to be late meeting us."

"You should've seen the look on his face when we told him it wasn't your birthday," said Red. "He was totally confused. We were, too."

From the looks her three BFFs were giving her, Snow knew that they were waiting for an explanation. "My stepmom has the fake mapestry I made," she told them and immediately had their attention. "It was in my blue bag when I went to take it out of my trunker after classes yesterday. Grandmother Enchantress sent it to me to give to her. And after I did my stepmom told me E.V.I.L. is suspicious of Wolfgang, so —"

"Yeah, he found out this morning he's been denied Society membership," Red told her.

Snow nodded. After what her stepmom had said about Wolfgang's "bad family," his rejection came as no surprise.

"So Ms. Wicked bought that your mapestry was the real one?" Rapunzel asked Snow.

"She did," Snow replied. "She also wants *me* to help her use it to find the treasure. Can you believe it?"

Snow could feel Red's gaze on her. She turned her head

164

until their eyes met. Speaking firmly, she said, "But there's no way I would *ever* work on the side of evil."

"Of course you wouldn't!" exclaimed Cinda.

"Goes without saying," added Rapunzel.

Snow leaned forward, still looking at Red. "You know that, too, don't you?"

"I . . . um . . ." Red stuttered. She gulped and started again. "I've never doubted you, not really," she said, her words rushing out at last. "But there's just so much at stake, and your stepmom *is* part of E.V.I.L. So Wolfgang warned me not to —"

"Not to trust me?" Snow interrupted.

"Well, just not *completely*," Red said lamely.

"Humpf," muttered Snow. "So you decided to trust *him* over *me*?"

Red raised an eyebrow. "You mean I'm only allowed to trust one of you?"

Snow hesitated. "Well, no." And come to think of it, Snow herself had mistrusted Wolfgang just as much as he'd apparently mistrusted her.

"I'm sorry," Red said, looking contrite. "I've been so afraid that Ms. Wicked might get you to tell her things we didn't want her to know."

Snow considered this. "My stepmom *can* be pretty persuasive," she admitted. "But I'd never tell her anything to jeopardize our mission to find the treasure, save the school, and defeat E.V.I.L."

"I believe you," said Red. She reached out to grasp one of Snow's hands. "Forgive me?"

"Yes," said Snow, sending her a sweet smile. "I do." She gave Red's hand a squeeze.

Cinda and Rapunzel exchanged a look of relief. "Well, thank grimmness for that!" Cinda exclaimed, which made everyone laugh.

"I wonder why Ms. Wicked asked *you* to help her find the treasure?" Cinda mused as their laughter ebbed. "Why not my stepsisters? They've done E.V.I.L.'s bidding before, after all."

Snow drew her legs up and wrapped both arms around her knees. "I don't think she wants E.V.I.L. to know about the mapestry. So that if she does find treasure, she can keep it for herself!" She shook her head. "And I didn't exactly rush in with an offer to help her. So to get back at me, she gave me a cupcake loaded with pieces of apple."

The other girls were outraged. "So that's what happened!" exclaimed Cinda. "That Ms. Wicked is even worse than my two Steps. She's evil to the *core*."

"Yeah," said Red. "As rotten as . . ."

"A rotten apple!" Rapunzel supplied.

Snow smiled at her friends and nodded. They were right. Her stepmom was just downright *mean*. She hadn't even come to visit her in the infirmary. Not that Snow *wanted* to see her, of course!

"Hey, why are we wasting our breath on her, anyway?" Cinda asked everyone. "Let's move on to fun stuff, if you know what I mean." She shot Rapunzel and Red a pointed look.

Snow sat up straighter, watching curiously as Red and Rapunzel went outside the door to her room. They were back in a moment, carrying a box that was bigger than Snow's feather-filled pillow. They set it on the bed.

"Ta-da! We brought something for you!" Red announced.

"Open it," said Cinda, and Snow did. Carefully, she parted the fragile sheets of white tissue. And inside, she discovered . . .

"A ball gown!" she said in surprise. An adorable and sparkly pale turquoise one, with puffed white sleeves striped with dark turquoise satin piping.

"Just because you're not allowed to go to the ball, doesn't mean you can't get all decked out for it," said Red.

Her spirits rising, Snow hopped from her bed. As the Grimm girls all hugged, tears fell from more than one eye. Happy tears of friendship.

"Thanks, you guys," Snow said softly. Then, with the help of her friends, she put on the cute gown. They'd even brought slippers. Digging deeper in the box, Snow exclaimed in surprise, "What a grimmorgeous tiara!"

All eyes swiveled toward the silver tiara she held. "Oh!" breathed Snow as she turned it round and round in her hands. It sparkled with turquoise jewels that had been clustered together to form seven four-leaf clovers. A big one at the center of the tiara, and three smaller ones on either side. How sweet! They all knew she missed her lucky clover amulet. But she hadn't thought her friends even knew that seven was her lucky number!

"It's *more* than grimmorgeous. It's grimmelegant!" Snow beamed at them. "You guys are the best," she told them. "Thank you *sooo* much times a million!"

Her three BFFs exchanged looks of confusion. "The tiara didn't come from any of us," Red insisted.

"But who else could have put it in the box?" asked Snow. Prince knew seven was her lucky number, but there was no way a boy would give a girl he hardly knew a costly gift like this. So who *had* given it to her?

"Check inside of it to see if it's engraved," Rapunzel suggested.

Snow did. "There *is* something written here." She squinted at the tiny lettering. "Seven Dwarves Jewelers," she read aloud.

"Never heard of it," said Red. None of the other girls knew of a jewelry store by that name in all of Grimmlandia, either.

It crossed Snow's mind that her stepmom could have planted the gift somehow. And remembering the blue shoelaces and the opal brush, she was tempted to toss the tiara away regardless of how beautiful it was.

"Look — here's something I missed. It must have fallen out of the box when I opened it." Snow's new gown made a crinkling sound as she bent over to pick up a small vellum card that had fallen to the floor. She read the words on the card aloud:

"Riding on high,
I trick the eye.
If you wish to fool,
Press my center jewel.
Where once was something,
will appear nothing."

"It's a riddle!" Snow exclaimed.

"Maybe the library gooseknob sent it," joked Rapunzel.

Snow giggled. But then a new idea struck her as she recalled that Red's magic basket and Cinda's glass slippers had been accompanied by riddles, too. She looked at her three BFFs. "Do you suppose this tiara could be my —"

" — magic charm?" Red finished excitedly.

"Oh my gosh, yes!" said Cinda, clapping her hands together.

"It's got to be!" echoed Rapunzel.

Snow stared at the tiara with fresh wonder, hardly able to believe it. Her very own magic charm! Though she still missed her lucky clover necklace, a *magic* charm seemed as good or even better than all of her lucky charms put together!

" 'Riding on high, I trick the eye,' " she repeated. Slowly, she lifted the tiara and placed it on top of her head. " 'If you wish to fool, press my center jewel.' " Reaching up, she pressed her finger against the largest cloverlike cluster of jewels.

Instantly, looks of alarm came into her three friends' eyes. Cinda's hands flew to her mouth. "She's gone!" she exclaimed.

"Can you hear me, Snow?" Red called out.

"Come back!" pleaded Rapunzel.

Quickly, Snow removed the tiara. "I was here all along," she assured them.

"But what just happened?" said Red.

A grin spread over Cinda's face. She repeated the second half of the riddle. " 'Where once was something, now appears nothing.' Get it?"

Red's jaw dropped. "Your magic charm made you invisible!"

Rapunzel laughed in delight.

Snow put the tiara on top of her head again, only this time she didn't press on the jewel. "Am I still here?" she

170

asked. Since she'd still been able to see herself even when she'd appeared invisible to her friends, she wasn't sure.

They nodded. "And you look grimmsolutely stunning in that gown and tiara!" added Red.

"That's for sure," said Rapunzel.

Cinda reached for the hand mirror, which lay on top of the bedside table, handing it to Snow. "Here," she said. "You can see for yourself."

"Well, well, well," said the talking mirror, whose ghostly image appeared as soon as Snow held the mirror up to her face. "This is an improvement! Looks like I underestimated those busy-bee dwarves. They came through for you again."

"Did you say dwarves or scarves?" Snow asked in confusion. She sat down on the edge of her bed, and her friends gathered around to stare at the mirror.

"Scarves? What are you talking about? I'm talking about the *dwarves* in your schoolbag," it explained. "They said they came from your handbook."

Snow's eyes widened as realization dawned. "I forgot to press the illustration in my Handbook to put them back inside their bubble after they helped me in History class on Wednesday! I guess they've been hanging out inside my bag and Handbook since then."

"Yes, and they've taken quite a shine to you," chuckled the mirror. "*Shine*. Ha! Ha! Get it?"

"Uh-huh, go on," said Snow.

"Didn't you notice them trying to be helpful? Handing you things every time you opened your bag?"

Snow thought about how things had seemed to jump into her hands each time she reached into her bag lately. And how she'd seen the bag wiggle or heard it make weird sounds. And there were the times she'd imagined she'd seen little hands waving to her, and a bearded face. Only it wasn't her imagination after all, it seemed! "Well, now that you mention it —"

"They stitched that tapestry thing, too," interrupted the talking mirror. "Kept me awake night and day with threads going every which-a-way."

"The mapestry?" said Snow. "But until the enchantress made it visible, they wouldn't have been able to see the threads because — Oh, wait," she said, interrupting herself. "The directions that came with the invisible twill said that it would be visible to only the stitcher — *or magical helpers in his or her employ.*"

"Ah! And since the dwarves were helping you, they were 'in your employ,'" Rapunzel concluded.

"Well, that explains why I couldn't remember sewing certain parts of the mapestry," Snow said. She looked sheepishly at her friends. "I thought maybe I'd been working on it in my sleep."

"Those dwarves have assigned themselves the task of watching over you," the talking mirror told her. "Wish I'd been in the bag to see how they finagled you that magic charm."

Snow's eyes lit up. "I need to thank them!"

Cinda reached onto the table again and handed over her blue bag. Snow opened it and peered inside. "Where are you, little dwarves?" she called out. Silence.

"Now that their work is done, they'll have gone back to your handbook to rest," said the mirror. "But if you ever need their help again —"

"I'll just open my handbook and call them out," Snow finished. "Thanks, guys," she called down into her bag. "For *everything*!" She wasn't quite sure, but she thought she heard some little voices call back, "You're welcome!"

By now, music from the Great Hall had begun to drift into the infirmary, which meant that the ball was starting. It was time for the girls to leave. After lots of hugs and good wishes for a swift recovery, Snow's friends said their farewells and dashed off in a whirl of silk and satin.

After they'd gone, Snow lay back on her bed with the tiara in her lap and closed her eyes, thinking. Wolfgang's failed attempt to infiltrate E.V.I.L. was a real blow. Getting information about the group's future plans was essential, and someone *inside* the Society at its meetings would be best placed to get that information. But if not Wolfgang, then . . . who?

Words that Ms. Wicked had spoken to her last night

floated into her mind: *"One day, I'm hoping that you'll come round to seeing things my way."* Her eyes flew open. Did she dare do what she was thinking of doing? Snow got goosebumps at the very thought. She wanted nothing more to do with her stepmom. Not ever! Yet who knew better than *she* how Ms. Wicked's mind worked?

No one, that's who! And with a little drama coaching from Red she might just pull off an act convincing enough to make her stepmom believe that she'd come round to seeing things her way after all. And if she got into the Society . . .

Snow sat up straighter. Did she really have the courage for this? Her glance fell on the jeweled tiara in her lap. Grandmother Enchantress had once told the Grimm girls that magical charms only came to those of good heart. Though the dwarves had had a hand in getting Snow hers, she still must have been judged worthy. So maybe she needed to start believing in herself, too. For surely a good heart was also a courageous heart! She only wished there was something she could do right this moment to help save the Academy, though.

Just then, from the corner of her eye, Snow saw a stick fly in through the infirmary window. Her head whipped around in surprise and she gasped. For it wasn't a stick after all. It was the Pied Piper's pipe!

15

Dancing

By now, the renegade pipe had a string of seven items dancing along behind it. The chess piece, the ruby ring, the spoon and silver dish, a necktie, an umbrella, and a fancy vase. Probably enough stuff to do a lot of damage to the protection surrounding Grimmlandia if they all escaped over the wall into the Nothingterror. Usually seven was Snow's lucky number, but this situation didn't seem lucky at all!

A flurry of notes floated through the air as the pipe and its followers flew out the infirmary door and down the hall. Snow stared after them, stunned. Then she leaped into action. After all, hadn't she just wished there was something she could do to help save the Academy? She had to catch that pipe!

Snow took off after the line of objects, following them through the hall, and up some stairs. She encountered no one on her mad dash. Except for her, the whole school was at the ball.

Eventually, she found herself all alone on the east-side balcony above the Great Hall where the Hickory Dickory Dock clock stood. She'd lost sight of the pipe and its followers! Down below in the Hall, dancers whirled and twirled. Luckily, without realizing it, she'd picked up the tiara from her lap as she left the infirmary and now held it in one hand. Sticking it on her head, Snow reached up and pressed the center jewel of her tiara to make herself invisible. After all, she had been told to stay in bed and she didn't really want everyone to see her with this rash if she could help it.

Snow scurried to the balcony and looked out over the transformed Hall, which had been readied for the ball. She sighed at its beauty. Huge swags of rich white satin hung around each window, fluttering in the cool night air that drifted in. The long meal tables had been replaced by smaller satin-draped ones, spaced here and there. A large crystal vase filled with white, pink, and red flowers and glittery stuff sat at the center of each tabletop. She sighed wistfully. If only she could be down there!

Suddenly, she caught sight of the pipe and its followers again! "Come here, you rotten pipe," she murmured under her breath.

As the pipe darted around the Hall near the ceiling — could it have been drawn here by the music? — Snow's eyes scanned the dancers below. Wolfgang had come, she saw. He and Red, along with Cinda and Prince Awesome, had formed a foursome to dance a simple country dance. She spotted Rapunzel, too, over by one of the snacks tables, chatting with Prince Foulsmell and another boy.

Where is Prince Prince? she wondered. This ball was in his honor, so he must be down there somewhere. She caught a flash of silver in the moonlight streaming in from a window. It was a coin, flipping through the air! She couldn't see who was flipping it, because of the streamers. But she could guess. *Prince.*

So far, it seemed that no one in the Hall had noticed the artifacts that swooped and looped through the air above them. Probably because it was hard to see them through the dozens and dozens of long decorative satin ribbon streamers that dangled from the ceiling. Snow frowned when she caught sight of her stepmom dipping a cup of punch from a large bowl. She was there as one of the chaperones, of course. When her hard eyes swept the room, Snow felt glad to be invisible!

Having whooshed around the Hall, the pipe and its followers now headed back toward the balcony. She'd lost sight of the objects for a moment, but now they swooped right past her. If only she could catch the pipe. But how? Her eyes searched the balcony for ideas. There! Hanging from the side of the Hickory Dickory Dock clock was a butterfly net. No, a bird-catching net. Because occasionally the cuckoo in the clock went cuckoo and had to be recaptured. She dashed over, grabbed the net, and waited.

Finally, the pipe circled back her way. Snow swung the net. *Swoosh!*

Caught! The minute the pipe was inside the net, it stopped making music. Its followers floated gently to the floor of the balcony all around her. Snow quickly knotted the net so the pipe couldn't escape, though it thrashed back and forth.

In the scuffle, her tiara tipped to one side and slipped off. She caught it in one hand and set it back atop of her head, hoping that no one — particularly her stepmom — had been looking up at the clock when the tiara fell off. Otherwise, someone might have caught a glimpse of her!

Minutes later, she was startled to hear footsteps. She pushed the center clover on her tiara again, just in case it was necessary to do it each time she put on the tiara to remain invisible. Learning how her magic charm worked would take some time! She looked over as Prince entered the balcony. "Need some help?" he called out softly, turning his head this way and that, trying to find her.

Snow froze. She could tell he couldn't see her. Should she just stay quiet until he left? Despite her pretty gown, she didn't exactly look her best right now. Her cheeks and neck were still pink and blotchy. She did not want him to see her like this. But she could use his help. To save the Academy!

"Yes!" she called softly. "I need help getting that pipe calmed down. And gathering up these other artifacts and taking them out of here."

"Huh? Snow, where are you?" Prince whirled around, still trying to locate her.

She couldn't help giggling at the confused look on his face. "It's my new magical charm. A tiara that makes me invisible."

"I see," said Prince. "Or rather, I *don't* see."

Snow giggled again. Then his eyes fell on the pipe. "You really caught it!"

She nodded. Remembering he couldn't see her, she added, "Yes."

As he kneeled and tied the pipe up more securely, she began gathering the other artifacts in a small pile by the clock. "I have something for you," he announced when they'd finished. Then he reached into his pocket and pulled out a silver chain. One with a clover amulet.

"My necklace!" Snow exclaimed joyfully. "Where did you find it?" When she kneeled and took it from him, it must have become invisible, too, because he looked to the floor as if fearing he'd dropped it. She saw at once that the clasp was broken. Happy to have it back, she kissed the amulet, then stood up and slipped the necklace into the pocket of her ball gown.

"I *didn't* find it, actually," Prince said. He was talking to her knees, the place where he'd last seen her necklace when she'd kneeled to take it from him a moment ago. "Mermily did," he went on. "It caught on her tail while she was out swimming in the Once Upon. Awesome, Foulsmell, and I happened to be practicing with the catapults on the riverbank just afterward. I offered to return it to you."

"Thank you so much!" Snow said gratefully. "But, um, I'm standing up now." After he scrambled hastily to his feet, she continued. "My friends and I went out to Maze Island a few days ago. It must have fallen into the river on the way." She'd have to remember to tell Red that apparently her basket couldn't fetch things that were underwater.

"It's Mermily you should thank," Prince said humbly.

"Yes, sure," Snow agreed. "I will."

Prince cocked his head in the direction of her voice. "It's a little weird to be talking to a disembodied voice. But if you'd rather not be *seen* with me . . ."

"That's not it," Snow said quickly. She knew she had a choice to make. She could let her vanity keep her invisible, or she could simply *show up*, regardless of the consequences. The latter choice was the courageous choice. Besides, vanity was a trait of her stepmother's that she had no wish to copy.

Slowly, she reached up with both hands and lifted off the jeweled tiara. "The doctor said I can go back to the dorm tomorrow. I know I still look awful, though," she said. She replaced the tiara on her head, but didn't press on the center jewel, so that she'd remain visible.

Prince smiled. "No. You look cute — I mean, good — I mean . . . um, want to dance?" He reached for her hand, looking a little uncertain.

A glance toward the knotted net showed her that the pipe had finally settled down. And those seven artifacts weren't going anywhere. She'd ask Prince to take all that stuff down to Principal R in a few minutes. But for now . . .

Snow smiled back at the prince and put her hand in his. She didn't need to be holding the magic hand mirror to know that the twinkle in his blue eyes and the smile on his face would perfectly match his reflection. The musicians in the far balcony began a new tune, and Snow placed her other hand on his shoulder.

And then Prince swept her up in the most perfect Happily Ever After dance ever, ever, ever!

As they whirled and twirled around the balcony, Snow found herself thinking about good and bad luck and how sometimes it wasn't so easy to tell the difference. After all, one *could* say it was *good* luck that she'd gotten a rash, since, despite being up in the balcony instead of downstairs in the Hall, she'd gotten to dance with Prince anyway.

Just then, Prince spun her around again, and she happened to glance over the balcony and catch her stepmother's eye. Ms. Wicked was craning her neck to squint up at her, and she did *not* look happy. *Well, so what?* thought Snow. Pretending she hadn't noticed her stepmom's scowl, Snow waved gaily to her. Which made her frown even more. *Well, ha-ha!*

The sign on Snow's armoire popped into her head: *Luck Comes to Those Who Are Prepared.* She'd always thought that being *prepared* meant having lots of lucky charms. But after all she'd been through in the last few days — sometimes with and sometimes without her lucky charms — she was no longer so sure. Of course, she'd still keep her lucky charm collection. (It would seem odd to be without them!) But there were other, more *active* ways of being prepared. Like studying before a big test, for example. Like making and keeping good friends who could support you even when your stepmother didn't. In a way, Red, Rapunzel, and Cinda were her *biggest* good luck charms.

She smiled to herself, picturing the look of amazement that was sure to come over her Grimm girl friends' faces when she told them what she'd decided to do. Volunteer to spy on E.V.I.L.! But all that would come later.

For now there was just this dance. And this prince. As she and Prince twirled around the balcony once more, Snow was *prepared* to enjoy it!

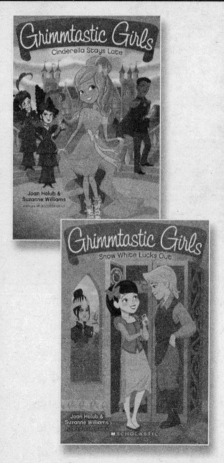

Rapunzel's magical fast-growing hair can be a nuisance, especially when an accident in Bespellings class gives it a case of the wiggles! But Rapunzel can't let her grimmorrible hair woes distract her — she and her friends, Cinda, Red, and Snow are putting on a school festival to help save Grimm Academy from the E.V.I.L. Society. Once Rapunzel tracks down her magic charm, she won't let a bad hair day get in the way of stopping E.V.I.L.!